Stra

by

Jeanette Basson

ACKNOWLEDGEMENTS

Thanks

To my husband James for your patience and understanding.

To my Mother. You gave me the strength to never give up on my dreams.

To my Daughter Angie. Without your help, this book would probably have never been completed.

To my Daughter Stephanie for hours of listening to me talk about and read passages of this book to her.

To my Granddaughter Savanah who was my encourager and cheerleader throughout this process.

To the Columbus Writer's Group. Thanks for the encouragement and advice.

Special Thanks

To Ron Donaghe who took on the challenge of editing this book and helping me through the publishing process. You had no idea what you were getting into. Thanks!

Prologue

Dear Diary

May 20

We've been on the river for four days. It's been such great fun laughing, singing, and acting as if we were teenagers again. It's still hard to believe we're actually in Alaska! Who would've guessed that I, forty-four-year-old Julie Stone, with my husband Paul, and Bo our dog would be in a boat, in the middle of the river, on our way to spend the summer working on an old run-down cabin that Paul had been dreaming about rebuilding for years. This has been the most romantic time of our lives.

The trip up was fantastic, and now these last few days on the river have been better than I could have ever dreamed possible. I can't wait to get to the cabin and actually set up our permanent campsite. I don't really care if we get the cabin rebuilt; I'm just enjoying having this time alone with Paul.

If I'd known what tragedy lay ahead, I would never have agreed to this trip. If only Paul had trusted me more. Oh Paul, why?

Chapter 1

A few weeks after our oldest son Todd's wedding, Paul came into the kitchen saying, "Julie, pack your things we're going to Alaska." I just stood and stared at him.

"And just when are we going to do this?" I asked.

He laughed, sounding delighted at my surprise. "Next month on the first day of May," he said. "I'm turning the business over to Todd," He explained. "He can run that hardware store as well as I can; he's practically been running it ever since he finished college. Now that he's married, you know how badly they'll need the bigger income. So, now is the year for us to take that vacation to Alaska that we've been planning for years."

A few winters ago, Paul had gone hunting in Alaska with some of his buddies. For months after he returned home all he could talk about was a cabin that was in the area where they camped, how beautiful Alaska was, and how badly that cabin needed to be repaired. He always said, if we ever had time, we were going back to rebuild that old cabin if at all possible. We'd always planned to go for a week or two, but we'd never had the time until now. I ran to him, threw my arms around his neck, and hugged him. "I'll pack our things!" I said, with a laugh.

Chapter 2

Paul had everything planned, even down to buying a new car. He gave his old truck to our youngest son Joey. "He'll need it since he's going to work on your parents farm for the summer," he said.

I wondered, just when and how he had time to plan all of this without talking it over with me or without me finding out. I guess I was just too busy with Todd's wedding to pay attention to what Paul was doing.

Paul said our new car rides like a dream, that it was much easier to drive, and it'll get much better gas mileage than the truck. He promised to let me drive part of the way, and I was so excited, I felt as if I would explode at any minute. He laughed and said the car would be completely broken in by the time we reached Anchorage.

We'd never had a vacation without the boys, until now. We've seen things we would've loved to show them, and it'll be fun telling them all that they missed, but I think we are both really enjoying this "just the two of us" trip. I'll have to remember to tell them, "Please don't wait until you're in your forties to take a trip like this."

We left our home in Seattle, about six o'clock on the first day of May. We didn't get very far the first few days, because we stopped to look at almost all the attractions from animal sideshows, to antique and junk shops, to any other tourist traps that caught our attention along the way. We had to keep reminding each other, not to buy anything because we wouldn't be able to take it with us and ourselves. But we told each other we could buy things on the way back home, if we went back home the same way that is.

Paul said, "We'll have to do better than this if we're going to make Alaska before winter." Paul was acting like he was twenty instead of forty-five. Although we've been married for twenty-five years, this trip was like the honeymoon we couldn't afford when we were first married. The time alone was so great. Just to be able to talk without interruptions has been wonderful. Without work, running here and there, and doing all the chores that we felt were so important that the days seemed to never end. We spent hours talking, singing, and sightseeing. We drove up through Canada to Anchorage, Alaska. I felt like we were dating again. I rode almost the entire way cuddled right next to Paul, him holding my hand most of the way.

Chapter 3

It took us almost two weeks to get to Anchorage because the roads were so terrible. In some places we had to detour more than once. Then there was the time we turned around backtracking, just to see some waterfalls. They were the most beautiful waterfalls we had ever seen. They looked like they were pouring right out of the sky. The falls were so tall and magnificent, it made us feel very small and insignificant. They completely took our breath away. Even though the side trip had taken up an entire day, we felt that it was well worth the time.

The camping became very monotonous, but the scenery was wonderful and exciting at the same time. We had many a romantic evening sitting snuggled close to each other watching our fire die down. We often saw bear and moose in the distance. One evening we watched a herd of about twenty caribou pass through a field close to us. They were a lot of fun to watch. Once we had to move our campsite because a moose just came walking right into our camp. I thanked God we were not completely set up. Moving as slowly as possible so we wouldn't spook him, we gathered our things, put them in the car, and drove on to the next campsite. Paul said it was only fair because it was his home first, and we were only visitors.

We almost always stopped when we came to a village or a small town for gas and food and any other thing we thought we might need. And of course, we always visited the local hardware store just to poke around in it and compare it to ours. Paul always had to talk with the owner about the business and swap stories. I loved to talk to the local people. It was fun to find out a little about the people and their towns. It amazed me how different we could be on some things, and how similar we were on others. Paul said we needed to be cautious when we were visiting with the people in town. He said not to be too specific about ourselves and where we were going because you never knew whom you were talking to. The locals usually told us where the best places to camp were, and a few times we even got a room in town for the night just to give us a break from camping. The food was always much better than our campfire meals, too.

I had never been this far away from home, and I was like a kid at Christmas time. The excitement of every day was like opening a new present. I wanted to experience everything, but I was impatient for what came next at the same time.

Chapter 4

When we finally reached Anchorage, we hired a floatplane to fly us to the outpost. The outpost was in a remote village and was the last place we would be able to buy supplies and rent a boat. According to our map, we would still be several days from our destination, and it would be our last contact with civilization for a little over three months.

Although Paul and I were very excited about flying to the outpost, Bo wasn't. He was so scared that we had to drag and push him onto the plane. Even with me sitting in the back with him trying to reassure him, and with him securely buckled in and firmly situated between my knees, he was still terrified. We'd been in the air for several minutes before he stopped whining and trembling and settled down. He just laid his head on my knee and pretended to sleep the rest of the way.

When we reached the outpost, we rented a boat and bought what supplies we hadn't brought with us. Even though we had made a list of everything we thought we would need, the storekeeper, who was also the outpost owner, took one look at it, took his pen, and marked through half my clothes, most of our books; he added much heavier coats, fur-lined gloves, and another toboggan for each of us. He told us where we were going was very rugged, and the weather was unpredictable. He said we would need more rope, another ax, extra saw blades, nails and another hammer, tarps, dried meat, dried beans, canned fruit, sugar, coffee, salt, and water purifier tablets just in case we couldn't find good drinking water. All the food had to be in tin cans or waterproof pouches and then wrapped securely in tarps.

After Paul and I, with the help of the outpost owner and his assistant had picked out things and packed them for travel. A couple of men approached Paul asking him where he was going and if he needed a guide. One of them had a strange, deep voice it made me turn and look at him. I was glad when Paul told him no that he knew where he was going. He continued to talk with Paul, saying if he changed his mind to let the outpost owner know. I heard that as I walked out and stood on the porch looking at the scenery. I must have taken a whole roll of film right there on the porch. Everything was just so beautiful. The sky was the brightest blue sky I had ever seen! Standing on the porch looking across the river I could see the reflection of all the trees and mountains in the water. It was spectacular! I just couldn't take it all in. I wanted to capture it all so I took my sketchbook and started sketching as quickly as I could, hoping that when we reach the cabin, I could find time to paint some of them.

Dear Diary

May 14
Although the trip has been fun for us, it has been pretty hard on Bo. As long as we were traveling in the car where we could stop every few hours to stretch our legs and let Bo run for a while, it wasn't so bad. But having to sit still in the plane, for almost an hour, not only made him nervous it also made him very stiff. But he's really making up for it now. He's running, rolling, and investigating everything. I don't blame him for running and carrying on. I almost wish I could do the same. The weather is just great. The air is so clear and light it makes me want to just raise my arms and whirl around like a child. I want to embrace it all, but I know there's no way to truly capture that feeling.

When I asked if it was safe for Bo to run lose the owner of the outpost said it would be safe as long as he didn't run into the woods. He said he didn't think there would be wolves or bears this close to the outpost during the day, but you just never could tell for sure. Sometimes, they would come in closer during the day if they were hungry, but they usually only came around late in the afternoon or at night. Sometimes they would get close just out of curiosity or pure orneriness, he said.

I got some terrific shots of Bo playing and acting so silly running down to the river and plunging in headfirst. He loved playing in the water and getting himself and anyone close to him totally wet like he did when he was a puppy. He would grab a stick and throw it over his back, then whirl around to grab it up again and run like he was playing ball. He was so cute. I just couldn't help laughing watching him. He absolutely loved the water, except for bath time that is. I sure hoped the pictures I'd taken turn out good. It would take the boys and Amy a year to go through all the snapshots because I'd already used quite a few rolls of film on the way up here. It would probably take me a year to have them all developed! I had to slow down, which made me think, *I only have five or six rolls left, but I just hate to miss anything. Maybe, I should ask Paul to add more film to our already mountain size pile of supplies. I guess I should first find out if the outpost carries the film*, I thought. *I can just hear his laughter now. Oh well, he'll just have to laugh.* I couldn't stand the thought of not being able to document this trip in every way I could. I couldn't possibly sketch it all, and I knew we'd never be able to take another trip like this, and that's why I knew I'd better capture these scenes while I could.

Chapter 5

The outpost though secluded was beautiful. It sat on a hill overlooking the river. There were three or four log cabins for rent, and a café and bar in the outpost, which served good food. I thought this was great. It gave us a break from my burned flapjacks and our campfire cooking.

We stayed in one of the cabins for two days while gathering our supplies and loading the boat. I commented that the cabin was nicely decorated with red and black striped blankets and throw pillows that had wolves and elk printed on them. I told Paul that I really liked the cabin even though it was just a basic cabin with only a bed, a table, and a couple of chairs. Paul laughed and said I'd better enjoy it because it was a mansion, compared to the one we were headed to.

We packed and repacked our supplies, checking things off our list trying to make sure we had all we thought we might possibly need for the next three and a half months. We didn't want to run out of anything. Finally, on the third morning, we put our boat in the water. As we pulled away from shore, I looked back thinking, how beautiful and peaceful the outpost looked in the morning light, with the mists rising off the water. I was so excited I could scarcely contain myself and Paul was smiling like a kid at Christmas.

Thank God, for the motorboat. I hated to think of having to paddle all the way as people had to do many years ago. Occasionally, Paul would turn the motor off, and we would silently float with the current. It was so peaceful without the sound of the motor, and he said it was good to conserve our fuel. We'd paddle into little beaches and small inlets to look at something strange or unusual that had caught our attention. We'd use these side trips to make coffee and eat lunch most of the time. I don't think there's anything that smells as wonderful as coffee brewing over a campfire. Even our sandwiches tasted better than they ever had, sitting there on the banks of that river.

While we ate our lunch, Bo would run around investigating everything. Once he had a close encounter with a porcupine. Thank God that he could still move fast when he needed to. Even with his quick reflexes, he got two porcupine quills in his nose because of his curiosity. By the sounds he was making, you would've thought we were killing him when we removed the quills. After that, he stuck to bringing sticks back for us to throw for him.

Even with the motor, it didn't seem like we made many miles each day. With almost twenty-four hours of daylight, we could've spent a lot of time on the water, but Paul said five or six hours in the boat was all his body could take. And he didn't want to run the motor too many hours at a time, because he was afraid it might overheat. When I asked how far it was to the cabin, he said, he thought it was at least a hundred miles from the outpost. And that it would take at least five or six days to reach it, depending on how many hours we spent on the water. I didn't complain about the slow progress. We were having fun and enjoying the scenery so much that we really didn't worry about the time. More than once he said, "Someday we might want to buy land in Alaska and build our own cabin." I just laughed at him telling him he knew he couldn't stay away from home or the boys that long.

Dear Diary

May 21
Unless I have some film buried somewhere in our supplies, I've already used well over half the rolls. Thank goodness the outpost had ten more rolls, and we had room for them in our packs. I need to make myself slow down. I really want to make sure I

have enough film to take before and after pictures of Paul's old run-down cabin.

We saw all kinds of wildlife playing along the banks of the river and in the water. Once we pulled in close to the shore just to watch a couple of otters playing and to let me sketch them. They were magnificent, funny little animals, and were such a delight to watch. They would climb out of the water run up the hill, and then slide back into the water on the very muddy slide they had made down the bank. I hoped someday to paint them. Bo thought they were really having fun too. He wanted so badly to get in the water so he could play with them. It was all Paul could do to keep him in the boat.

Seeing the animals in the wild was just incredible, and the water and air were so clear I could see up the river for what seemed like miles. But Paul said the distances could be deceiving because you could see so far. What looked to be a mile or two could be ten.

Once, we laughed so hard and got such a kick out of watching a mother bear spank her cub for getting in the water. Paul said it reminded him of when I would spank Joey for playing in the water. He just could not stay out of the water. If there was even the tiniest puddle of water close by, he was in it, no matter how he was dressed.

At first, Bo grumbled and growled out of frustration and wanting to get out of the boat to chase the animals, but he soon grew tired of being told no. Once the *new* wore off, he spent most of his days lying in the bottom of the boat and sleeping.

The scenery was like looking at photos in a wildlife book. Everything was just breathtaking. It was so beautiful. I'm sure if I could have turned my head like an owl I would have. Paul, laughed, saying I was surely going to twist my head off trying to see everything at once, and that I would have a permanent crick in my neck if I didn't stop.

Chapter 6

It was our fourth day on the water and the weather was excellent. There was just enough of a breeze blowing to make me lift my face to it. It was only one o'clock, but we were putting into shore early. Paul thought something was wrong with the boat's motor, or maybe the gas line was clogged. Either way, Paul wanted to check it out. There was a good beach here, and it might be quite some time before we found another one. I told Paul I wouldn't complain that it would be nice to have a little extra time to rest and explore the area. "Who knows this might be just the place to buy and build our own cabin," I said, laughing.

There were lots of rocks and boulders bordering each end of the beach, but it was the best place we'd seen in quite a while. Paul didn't want to pull into a bank where there was no area to pull the boat up onto land, and this was the only place we'd found that had a good spot to do that. While Paul was checking the motor, I picked up my camera and sketchbook. Paul reminded me to take my rifle with me if I was going exploring. I slung the strap over my shoulder and went in search of a place to set up camp. I still felt foolish carrying the gun with me, but Paul said we should always be prepared to defend ourselves because a bear or any other animal could be around the next bush and we had to be ready.

Poor old Bo was so glad to be out of the boat, he jumped out the minute the boat pulled onto the beach. He ran all around the beach not knowing which way to go first. He would run down the beach as fast as he could and whirl around slinging dirt behind him. Then he would run back to me with his tongue hanging out. It looked like he was laughing; he was so happy to be on land again. Finally, he just lay down and rolled in the sand. Laughing, I thought that that looked like such fun. The sand looked so inviting, I wished I could just lie down on it and look up at the sky.

You would've thought Bo was a puppy by the way he was acting. There have been times on this trip when I felt sorry about bringing him with us. Paul didn't want to bring him because he is about eight years old, and Paul thought the trip might be too much for him. But, after much debating, Bo came with us. I just couldn't leave him behind. He's always been my dog, and we've never been separated for more than a day or two. I just couldn't stand the thought of leaving him for almost four months.

The boys and I found Bo on a country road where someone had abandoned him. He didn't look to be much more than three or four months old. The poor, little thing looked half-starved just sitting there on the side of that old dirt road like he was waiting for us. When we stopped and got out, he ran to me, sat down on my foot, and looked up at me with those big sad eyes as if to say, "Where have you been, I've been waiting for you." And from that moment on he was my dog. When we got home, Paul laughed and laughed. "Julie, that's just about the ugliest little dog I have ever seen." He looks like some old gray-haired man that hasn't combed his hair or his beard for weeks. But I assured him it wasn't anything a good bath and brushing and some food couldn't take care of. That was about eight years ago. The boys named him Bo. He loves Paul and the boys, and they had many adventures playing ball and rough housing together. He followed the boys almost everywhere they went. He also spent many a night sleeping in Paul's lap, waiting for me to finally finish the housework for the night so he could have mine. Even when he was with them, he always knew where I was. He's turned out to be a very loyal companion to the whole family, but he's always been my dog.

While Paul continued working on the motor, I explored the beach for the best place to set up our campsite. I was hoping to find it quickly so I would have time to take some pictures and maybe do a little sketching before we started setting up the tent for the night. I found a good spot at the top of the beach. It was flat with a big enough area for the tent and a good-sized fire pit. I had just started into the woods to gather wood for our campfire when I heard Paul calling me. As I turned, I could see him lying halfway in the water on the rocks by the boat. Laughing, I stood with my hands on my hips and told him that I wouldn't fall for that old trick again. "I've been fooled by you too many times," I called. I just knew he was going to try to pull me into the water like he had done so many times before. As I started back, I could see that Bo had beaten me to Paul and he was running around and around pawing at him. He was whining and trying to pull him out of the water. I called out to Paul, knowing that at any minute he would sit up and laugh, but he didn't. All at once I knew something was really wrong! I ran to him as fast as I could, dropped down by him, calling his name, shaking him, and hoping he would open his eyes and laugh at me for being so scared!

Chapter 7

No, No, No! Paul is dead! Dead! Lord, he can't be dead! This can't be real. He was alive just a few minutes ago! "Please God. No!" I screamed.

I tried everything, I even gave him CPR, but nothing worked! I just knelt there, shaking him and telling him to wake up! I sat there shaking him, calling for help, thinking surely someone would come to help, but of course, nobody came. All the while I was silently praying, "Please Lord, please send someone to help me! Please let this be a nightmare! Please. Oh please, God, don't take Paul away from me" I cried. "Please don't leave me out here alone! Oh, Lord. Please don't do this to me"! I frantically looked around, thinking I heard someone screaming! I listened intently to see who it was, and then I realized it was me! I covered my face with my hands, sobbing, praying that I would wake up and that this would all just be a horrible dream! Finally, after what seemed like days, I had to accept that this was real. Paul was dead. I was alone. "Oh, God, what am I going to do?" I asked.

Paul's feet and legs were still in the water, so I took him by the arms and started pulling him up onto the shore. That's when I saw a little bottle in his hand. My hands shook as I reached for that tiny dark bottle. Taking the bottle from his hand, I knew what it was even before I read the label. *Nitroglycerin!* "Paul? Why would you need nitroglycerin?" I asked. "Oh, Paul, how could you deliberately keep this from me! We have never kept secrets from each other! Why didn't you tell me, Paul? Why, oh why?" I kept asking him. "If you had only let me know, I could have helped you! Oh, Paul!"

I don't know how long I kept asking him this, but finally, I realized that I understood why. He knew that I would never have agreed to this trip had I known. He knew this trip was as much my dream as it was his. He would've done anything to make this trip happen, even keeping something like this from me. "Oh, Paul, you should've told me anyway. Don't you know you meant more to me than any trip? I could have helped you. We could've worked this out. Oh, God, why didn't you tell me, Paul, why?"

I sat by Paul all night, crying and talking to him not knowing what else to do. I was so angry one moment and so hurt and scared the next! How could God let this happen? How could Paul let this happen? I was so mad at both of them! I just sat there sobbing telling God how angry I was and asking Him why. I kept telling myself this couldn't be right. I laid my head on Paul's chest willing him to breathe. I kept telling him to breathe, to please just breathe. I said, "You can't be dead. We had plans. We were going to rebuild the cabin." I shook him, telling him to wake up. "Don't you do this, Paul!" I cried. "Don't you dare leave Bo and me here by ourselves! We need you! We can't survive without you! Please! Please! Oh please, Paul, wake up! I love you! I need you!"

"How can I handle this Lord?!" I asked again and again.

The sun would soon be up, and I knew what I had to do. I laid my head on Paul's chest, sobbing, I told him goodbye. I turned to Bo and hugged him. I told him what a good dog he'd been for staying by me all night. Suddenly, I realized how cold I was. I knew I needed to get up and move, but I didn't want to leave Paul. Eventually, I got up and took Bo with me to gather some wood. I built a fire up closer to the trees at the top of the beach. I fed Bo and automatically made coffee and toast for myself like I did every morning. Even though I wasn't hungry, I knew I must eat.

Sitting by the fire, I reached into my pocket and took out my diary and the camera. I knew I must keep a record of what had happened, so I took my camera, and returned to Paul. Then I began to take pictures. They may be so blurry that no one will be able to recognize him because I was trembling and sobbing so hard. As I stood there, my legs almost gave way, but I gritted my teeth knowing that I must do this.

I realized it was important to continue keeping a daily record, even if I only wrote down the date each day. It would help me keep up with the time as it passed. But how could I write this? If I wrote this down, I would know it was real. Paul would truly be dead. I just sat there crying, unable to stop. Maybe writing it down would help keep me from going crazy, and it would be a record for the boys. The boys! "Oh, Dear God, how can I tell them about their dad?" I asked. How could I ever explain this to them? It's more than I can do. "Please, please, Lord Jesus, don't make me do this! I just can't! I can't!"

Chapter 8

I buried Paul today. I found a place, not too far in the woods, where the ground was soft enough to dig a grave. It's only a few feet deep because the ground below is still frozen. I had forgotten about the permafrost. Before wrapping Paul in a tarp, I wrote a letter explaining what had happened, who he was, and who to notify, if the grave was ever found. I know the message will be hard to read because my hands were trembling badly, and I could hardly see through the tears. I placed the letter in the pocket of his shirt with the top barely showing. I felt a little foolish for doing this, but I wanted to make sure if someone found his grave, they would know what happened. I also thought that I needed to do this in case I didn't make it back home either.

Oh, God, I had never done anything so hard in all my life! I can't tell you how agonizing it was to drag Paul's body, wrapped only in a tarp, all that way across the beach. The act of placing him in that grave almost ripped out my heart. I kept telling myself, "You must do this, Julie. There's no one else to bury him." But when I had to lower him into that shallow grave, my heart hurt so badly I thought I would surely die. A part of me hoped I would, just so the entire ordeal would be over.

I stood looking down in the grave at the brown tarp that wrapped Paul's body, and I broke down all over again. Oh, how I wished there had been a coffin! I kept telling God that the tarp wasn't nearly enough protection. Paul deserved more than that flimsy covering. Once again, I prayed for this to all be some terrible nightmare. "Please, oh please, Lord, let me wake up! Please just make this all go away!"

It took me a long time to cover Paul's grave because with every shovel of dirt I felt as if a knife was piercing my heart and I couldn't catch my breath. I thought that surely I would die and kept wishing that I would. I so wanted to be in that grave with Paul.

Sobbing and trembling, I just stood looking down at his grave. I kept telling God that I couldn't bear this. I asked Him repeatedly, "What will I do? How will I survive without Paul? It's not fair, God," I screamed. "You should have taken me too! How can you leave me here alone? I don't know anything about this place! I don't even think I can set up the tent by myself! What am I supposed to do now, God?"

I needed to make a marker for Paul's grave, even if it was only a cross made of two sticks. *I will try to make a more proper one later,*

I told myself. When I finished the cross, I decided to cover Paul's grave with stones. I couldn't bear the thought of some animal digging into it. When the grave was covered with stones, I found five smaller stones that were lighter in color than the others and placed them in a V shape on his grave. This way, if I don't survive, the boys will recognize their dad's sign when they come searching for us. If they find the grave, they will know its Paul's sign because of the V.

Chapter 9

Paul was the only man I'd ever loved. I'd loved him since I was twelve years old! I remember the first time I saw him, really saw him. My heart just skipped a beat. It was August, and he had come to help pick the fall apples on our farm. He was thirteen, and I just couldn't stop watching him. I was supposed to be helping peel and thinly slice the apples for drying and canning, but I kept messing them up because I was thinking about Paul. My grandma threatened to tie me to the chair if I didn't stay in the kitchen and help instead of running outside to watch the guys picking apples. Paul told me a few years later that he couldn't stop watching me either. He said he almost fell off the ladder watching me. He told me that from then on, he knew someday he would marry me and that the thought of it almost scared him to death.

I was so young and foolish then. Every time my family would go to town, I would make an excuse to go into his father's hardware store where he worked just so I could catch a glimpse of him. My dad would always tease me and ask if I was able to find what I was looking for at the hardware store. He and mom always knew what I went there for. We very seldom said a word to each other. We just spent the time sneaking glances at each other. But, when he turned sixteen and had gotten his first car, he asked me out on a date. Of course, I said yes. And we've been together ever since.

I was eighteen, and he was nineteen when we married. It was the happiest day of my life. I thought I would surely pass out. My mother kept telling me to calm down and breathe, that everything would be all right. Paul was so shy, he said he thought of everything he could to keep from standing in front of all those people in the church. He was so nervous he even thought of kidnapping me and running away to get married. He said that even though he was scared to death and was sure he would make a complete mess out of everything, the thought of not marrying me made him gather his strength and go through with the wedding. We were so silly and so much in love.

"God, how can I survive without him? What will I do, God? Please, God, I need someone to tell me what to do next. Please don't leave me here alone. Please send someone to rescue me. Please, oh please, Lord, don't do this to me!"

Chapter 10

After I finished the terribly agonizing task of burying Paul, I felt as if my heart was breaking all over again. I could hardly breathe. As I stood there, looking down at the grave, all at once I was furious at God and at Paul! In a blind rage, I reached down and grabbed up fistfuls of dirt! I wanted to dig him out of that grave, I wanted to see him one more time, I needed to touch his face and hold him. I felt so incredibly helpless. I kept reaching down taking fistfuls of dirt squeezing it into balls. Then all at once, I started throwing them at Paul's grave! Screaming and crying, I yelled, "This is your fault, God! This is your fault! But I will survive, God, I will survive! Do you hear me, God? I have to for the boys!" The boys! Oh, Dear Lord! "How can I tell them about their dad?" I asked, as I collapsed across the grave weeping and exhausted.

It was late by the time I had finished burying Paul. The fire that I had built earlier was out, so I gathered more wood and restarted it. After feeding Bo, I went to the boat thinking maybe I could fix the motor. I gathered up everything I could find, and carefully laid it all out by the engine. But, standing in the fading light looking at all the parts, I knew that I didn't even know where to begin. How I wished I had stayed with Paul. Maybe I would've known what to do had I watched him take it apart. Perhaps I could have saved him. Perhaps I could've given him the nitroglycerin and CPR if I had stayed closer to the boat instead of wandering around the beach thinking of sketching things and taking pictures. Maybe if I had paid more attention to Paul, I would have seen signs and could have gotten to him in time. Oh, God, maybe I could have saved him. Maybe. Oh, Lord, maybe there are just too many maybes.

Dear Diary

May 26

I had been so proud of myself when my friend Susan and I took a survival class at the Red Cross center. They taught us how to do CPR and what the warning signs of a heart attack or a stroke are. We learned how to help someone who was drowning, and how to use a splint to set a broken bone. I felt like I was entirely ready for any health emergency that I might run into, but I couldn't save Paul. If only I had I been there. Oh, Dear God, I might have saved him! Oh, I can't stand that thought. Lord, please help me!

Chapter 11

I stood there trembling and looking around when I suddenly realized that I was really alone. I was truly and completely stranded! I couldn't paddle the boat back to the outpost by myself. It would be upstream all the way. There were also many streams that fed into the river. Some of them were almost as big as the river was. What if I accidentally took one of them instead of staying on the river? I could end up even more lost than I already was. I might end up in a village, or I might just paddle for days getting deeper and deeper into the Alaskan bush. If only I had a map, I might have been able to follow it overland. We had one for the trip up to the outpost, but we had left it in the car in Anchorage. The man at the outpost said he would draw one for us, but Paul said he knew the way from there to the cabin. I should have insisted that we make a map to the cabin. *Oh, Lord, why hadn't I insisted on a map?*

I was terrified! I knew I would have to stay here until someone came to rescue me. *Oh, Julie, you must not panic! You must remain calm!* I kept telling myself this, over and over, but I kept finding myself frantically looking around. Every little noise or rustling in the bushes made me jump. I was so scared I just stood there trembling. I wrapped my arms tightly around myself trying to keep from falling apart. I knew that if there was anything out there, Bo would let me know, but what if it was too late? What if a bear or wolves came? At the thought of that, I turned and reached into the boat getting my rifle and checking to see if it was loaded. *Oh, Paul*, I thought, *thank you for making sure I always kept the guns close by.* I realized I had automatically kept the rifle with me throughout the entire ordeal of burying Paul. I told myself at least I could defend us. But I just couldn't seem to stay calm for more than a few minutes at a time. "Stop this!" I told myself over and over. Panic wasn't helping the situation at all. I'd never been a panicky person, and I was not going to start being one now! I pulled the small bag that held my pistol out of the boat and opened it. I took my pistol out and made sure that it was loaded, and then, strapping the belt and holster around my waist, I put the pistol firmly in place. This calmed my nerves a little. The pistol was heavy, but it felt good having it right there on my hip where I could grab it faster than I could the rifle. I didn't know it then, but the pistol would soon become a part of my daily wardrobe.

I needed to find a place for our camp that wasn't too far from the beach. I figured the small tent would work for now. I didn't even know if I would be able to set up the big tent by myself because Paul and the boys had always taken care of that. I just had to figure it out because there was no one to help me. I knew how to set up the small tent we used for the nights we were traveling but it wouldn't be enough shelter for long. "Oh, Julie," I told myself. "You've got to do this. Stop feeling sorry for yourself and get on with it." Blinking away fresh tears, I realized it was much later than I thought. When I looked at my watch, I saw it was nearly midnight. I would barely have time to get the small tent up before it was too dark to see what I was doing.

As I took the tent from the boat, I realized the boat was not secured very well. It only had a small rope tied around a large rock. Paul hadn't taken the time to anchor it better because we hadn't planned on being there long. What if it had drifted away in the night, or even earlier today? "Julie, you should've been paying more attention." I told myself. "Paul is not here to do everything for you. All this is now your responsibility!" I pushed the boat farther up onto the shore and took out the anchor. I stretched the rope far up on the beach and drove the anchor deep into the ground. I took another line and secured the back of the boat to a large rock. Now the boat was sideways to the shore. This would also make it easier for me to unload. I realized I needed to pay more attention to everything now and be more careful. I took the small tent and went to Paul's grave. I had decided I would set the tent up beside it. It would be a good place for the night anyway. And tomorrow I would look for a more suitable location.

Chapter 12

The next morning, I knew I had to get everything out of the boat. Thank the Lord I noticed that it wasn't anchored properly and took the time to do it last night. *Dear Lord, just the thought of losing all our supplies on top of being stranded makes me tremble with fear.* When I started unloading the boat, everything I moved reminded me of Paul, of how we had decided to bring this thing or that thing. Again, I felt as if my heart would explode. I couldn't seem to catch my breath or stop crying. I just sat there in the sand crying, hugging Paul's jacket to me. I felt lost, scared, and sorry for myself all over again.

But all at once, I was furious with Paul and with myself! I jumped up, grabbed the big tent, and pulled it from the boat. I would not let this beat me! I had to survive! I could hear Paul laughing at me. "That's my Julie," he would say. If he ever needed me to do something I didn't want to, or I thought I couldn't, all he had to do was make me mad. Then I could do anything. Well, I was plenty mad! So, I guess he was right! "I will do this, Paul Stone, one way or another!" I growled between gritted teeth.

I went back to the boat and started grabbing things and hauling them up to the fire.

There was no telling how many trips I made, but I finally had everything out of the boat. When I looked at all the packages, tarps, tools, and suitcases scattered all around I let out a huge groan. The area around the fire looked like a tornado had come through. There was no order to anything.

By the time the boat was empty, it was early evening. I couldn't believe it. Suddenly, I was exhausted! Thank goodness the small tent was up and the cot and sleeping bag were already inside. I was so tired, so after feeding Bo and myself, we crawled into the tent. I barely remember lying down and immediately fell into a deep, exhausted sleep. I didn't wake up until late the next afternoon.

I woke with a start. I remembered that all our supplies were still on the beach, and I began to panic. I had to find a place where I could put them out of the weather so they would be safe. I decided I would bring everything to the area around my tent so I could keep an cye on it. After I had made quite a few trips, I decided to store as much of the food as possible in the tent. I filled the tent so full, there was barely enough room for Bo and me to crawl in and sleep. I stretched out the largest tarp and placed the rest of the supplies in the middle of it. When I had everything in place, I folded the sides in to secure everything, and keep it as dry as possible. I then stretched one of the other tarps over the top to keep any water from seeping inside. While making the last trip to check on the boat, and put out the fire, I thought I heard voices up the river!

Chapter 13

I was so excited I started to shout for help, but I could almost hear Paul saying, *"Find out who it is, Julie, and know who you're dealing with first."* I was trembling with anticipation and relief, as I fastened the leash to Bo's collar. I silently thanked God that Bo wasn't a barking dog. Then as quickly and quietly as possible I ran down our beach. When we came to the boulders at the end of the beach, I put my finger to my lips and took hold of his collar letting him know to be quiet. Standing there I could barely hear the voices, and I couldn't tell how far up the river they were, but they were there! I could smell the smoke from their fire. I hadn't imagined the voices after all!

I started to climb up and over the boulders to see if I could find out where they were, but as I strained to listen, I knew that one of them was a man we had run into at the outpost. He was the man who had tried to get Paul to hire him as our guide. He had such a strange deep voice that I would know it anywhere. Paul had told him that we didn't need a guide, and I remember being glad that we hadn't hired him. As I listened, he was telling the other man that they should overtake us by tomorrow. The other man laughed, and then he said, "You know people die on the river all the time." *My Lord*, I thought, *they are planning to kill us!* But the man with the deep voice said no, that he would not be part of a killing. They were just going to rob us, sink the boat, and leave us in the woods. He said, "By the time they find their way back to the outpost, if they find the way back, we'll be back in the lower, forty-eight and home free."

I was too afraid to move. I just stood there for a few minutes holding on to Bo's collar. "Oh Lord," I prayed. "Please don't let them come past here until I can get everything hidden." Finally, I eased back from the boulder, and being as quiet as possible, we quickly made our way back to camp. I put out what was left of our fire and rubbed out all signs of it, praying that they had not smelled my smoke. I knew the men would be able to see our camp from the river, so working as quickly as I could I took down the tent wishing I had not stored so much in it. I began moving everything farther into the woods. I didn't unpack the tent or the tarp I just pulled them as far as I could into the trees. When I had finished that, I remembered the boat and knew it had to be hidden.

I ran down to the boat and gathered up all the loose parts of the engine, carefully putting them in my pocket. I made sure I got every little spring and screw that I could find. I thought about removing the motor, but I decided it would make too much noise. I knew I couldn't pull the boat up to the tree line with my own strength, so I grabbed a rope and rigged up a pulley system. I tied the rope to the end of the boat, then ran the rope around a tree, and tied the other end around my waist. After a lot of pushing and pulling, I finally managed to get the boat up to the trees. It seemed to take forever. I had to stop several times to move rocks out of the way, because when the boat would hit a rock, it sounded like someone was ringing a bell. I just kept praying that the men wouldn't hear the noise.

My back felt as if it was broken, but I knew I couldn't rest yet. Using limbs and brush, I covered the boat the best I could. Then, I took a pine branch that had a lot of needles on it and brushed out all signs of the boat and the campsite along with my and Bo's tracks. After I had hidden the boat, I went back to the area where I had dragged the tent and tarp. I quickly covered them with as much brush as I could gather. I also covered Paul's grave. I was trying to wipe out all signs that anything in this area was new or had been recently disturbed.

While I was hiding everything, I thought of when my brother Robbie, our cousins, and I played Cowboys and Indians when we were kids.

We had a lot of fun hiding from each other. I was very good at it back then, I thought, but this was no game, and I was not playing! It was almost dawn by the time I got everything hidden, and all signs brushed out.

After feeding Bo, who had lain all night quietly watching me, I made a cup of cold coffee for myself and ate some jerky. I sat down by Paul's grave. I was so tired and sleepy, but I was afraid to close my eyes thinking I might go to sleep and the men might come ashore and find me. So, I pulled Bo close to me whispering softly to him and waited, hoping and praying that I had done enough.

Just before dawn, I took the binoculars, and we moved from Paul's grave to an area behind the boat, where Bo and I lay in wait. Watching as the sun came up, we waited for what seemed like an eternity. Finally, the men came around the boulders. I trembled with fear holding my breath as I silently watched. I realized why we hadn't heard them earlier. They were using paddles. I could see they had a motor on their boat, but they weren't using it. They were almost silent. I guess they wanted the element of surprise, by traveling as quietly as they could. I put my hand on Bo to let him know to be very still, and then I took the binoculars and watched them. I wanted to make sure I would recognize both if I should ever see them again. I lay there hidden, watching until they were only a small dot in the distance.

Chapter 14

I don't know how long I lay there, but I had fallen asleep at some point because the sun was in the west when I woke up. Good old Bo was right there beside me. When I sat up, I realized how cold and stiff I was. With a hug, I told Bo what a good boy he was and promised him food. After he ate, we went in search of a new place to set up camp and build a fire. I would need to put the small tent back up. And I would need to make sure to build the fire ring under a tree and use the driest wood I could find so the smoke wouldn't be seen.

I found a place to set up the tent not too far from Paul's grave, but far enough away that no one could see it from the river. I cleaned the area and set up the tent after I had pulled everything out of it. I quickly reorganized all my supplies and bedding because I didn't want to have to do this before I went to bed for the night. Then I made a fire ring and built a fire just large enough to fix some food for Bo and me, even though I might not be able to eat a bite. All I was really able to do was sit and shiver with fear and cold.

I couldn't get Bo to come away from Paul's grave. So, I took his food along with my coffee and some crackers with cheese for me, and we sat by Paul's grave to eat. I surprised myself by eating everything. I hadn't realized how hungry I was. I knew I needed to eat on a more regular schedule if Bo and I were going to survive. I had to keep my strength up. I sat by Paul's grave for a long time before finally getting up, going back to camp, and putting more wood on the fire. I went into the tent and lay down on my cot feeling both mentally and physically exhausted. I thought I would rest for a few minutes thinking it would soon be time to make Bo come inside. I was afraid to leave him outside without knowing if there might be wolves or other animals around that might hurt him.

I must have fallen asleep because when I woke the sun was high in the sky. I jumped up and ran out of the tent looking for Bo. When I saw him still lying on Paul's grave, keeping guard, I just fell to my knees, covered my face and cried. I thanked God for keeping him safe. I must be more careful I told myself as I went to Bo telling him what a good boy he was. He wouldn't leave Paul's grave when I called, so I had to fasten the leash to his collar and lead him back to the tent. When we got inside, I made sure to zip it up behind me. I didn't want Bo to get out or anything else to get in. After drinking the last of the coffee and giving Bo his supper. I lay back down on the cot and tried to think of what to do next. I needed to make a plan.

Chapter 15

I slept the rest of that day and all that night. When I awoke, at first, I didn't know where I was. I quickly sat up, and all of a sudden everything came back in a flash. I buried my face in my hands and sobbed. Once again, I begged God. "Please just let this be a bad dream. Please don't let this be real. I don't know what to do. Lord, what will I do? How will Bo and I survive? No one knows where we are! The boys won't even look for us until September! I am so afraid! How will I protect Bo and myself? What if there are wolves in this area? I can't stand this, Lord! Please make this go away!"

I cried until Bo started whining and washing my face and pushing me with his nose. He never could stand to see anyone cry. When the boys were little and cried for any reason, Bo would whine and try to wash their faces until they stopped crying. Thank God, we brought Bo with us. Even though I knew he couldn't talk to me, I could talk to him, and he made me feel much safer.

I knew Bo didn't understand what had happened. I had to almost drag him away from Paul's grave. He just didn't want to leave. He kept looking back with his tail between his legs and a worried look on his face. I think he was confused or thought he had done something wrong. I bowed, my head. "Oh Lord, what would I have done here by myself?"

As I dried my eyes, I ran my hands through my hair and realized that I hadn't brushed it since this nightmare began. Nor had I washed my face, brushed my teeth, or had a bath. I told myself this would not happen again. Even though I was here alone, I had to do just like I did at home, which meant getting up each morning reading my Bible, making coffee and breakfast, getting dressed for the day, and writing in my diary, if only the date.

I rambled through my backpack to find my brush and brushed my hair. I went to where I had hidden our supplies and found a couple of buckets. Then I took my gun, the binoculars, and the buckets down to the river for water. I was very careful to look through the binoculars to make sure there was no one around. I also made sure that I walked on the rocks around the boulders so I wouldn't leave any tracks, as I went to and from the river. I filled my buckets and headed back to camp. Soon this became one of my daily routines. I would carefully walk on the rocks around the boulders and gather water at least a couple of times a day. I kept watch because I thought that the men would probably be coming back this way and I wanted to make sure that I saw them first.

After bathing and changing into clean clothes, I made coffee, cooked flapjacks, beans, and a can of beef hash for our breakfast. That was just about the best food I had ever eaten. And it was the most either one of us had eaten in days. After I washed the dishes, I took the scraps of food well away from camp and buried them so that the smell wouldn't attract any animals. This had always been one of our rules when we went camping. Paul said he didn't want to share our campsite with mice or bears, and the best way to keep them away was to keep the food and trash away from the tent area. We also made sure we thoroughly cleaned up our site when we left. We always tried to leave the area cleaner than it was when we got there. I made sure everything else was safe and secure. Then I just sat by the fire trying to plan what to do next.

I was so nervous I jumped at every little sound, thinking it might be a bear or maybe those men. I kept telling myself that I must stay calm, but it didn't seem to help. After going to Paul's grave, I took the binoculars and went to a place where I could hide and watch the river. With Bo beside me, I stood scanning the river watching for the men. Finally, I went back to camp put out the fire and went inside even though it was only seven o'clock and the sun was still up. It never really got dark at that time of year, so it didn't matter when I went to bed, it would still be light outside. I zipped the tent up, and then placed a stool, with a few pots on it, in front of the door. This way if anything tried to come in or Bo tried to get outside, to chase after something he had heard, I would hopefully hear the noise and have time to get my gun. After I had set up my alarm system, Bo and I went to bed.

Dear Diary

May 28

It's been five days since Paul's death, and as I've done every day since burying him, I went to his grave. Then I took the binoculars and the rifle to my lookout at the edge of the woods. Of course, I always have my pistol fastened around my waist just in case something gets close enough that I must use it instead. As I stood where I hoped no one could see me, I scanned the river for any sign of the men. So far, thank God, I haven't seen anything. I pray they've given up and taken another route back to the outpost, but I can't count on that. So, I stand and watch.

My plan for the day is to make sure this is the best place for our permanent camp before I try to set up the big tent. Knowing it'll be at least three months before we'll be missed, I'll need to get the big tent up so there will be enough room to keep my supplies dry, safe, and as secure as possible. The small tent is barely large enough for my cot and Bo, and most of the food. The rest of the supplies, I wrapped in a tarp and stored under the boat, but they'll not last long stored this way. There's too much rain and too many small animals that can easily get into the packages and spoil whatever is inside.

Chapter 16

Paul and I had called the boys while we were in Anchorage. We told them that we'd call them on September seventh at eight o'clock in the evening to let them know what time we'd start home and that we were okay. It had worked out perfectly for Todd and Amy to stay at our house while we were gone. They'd been married just a few weeks when we left for Alaska. Todd and Amy told us not to worry about a thing. They promised us they would take care of everything at the hardware store and the house. They even offered to keep Bo. I'm so glad now that we hadn't taken them up on that offer. I would be lost without Bo.

Joey was working for the summer on my parents' farm before he went back to college. He was in his junior year and studying Marketing and Business Management. He planned to manage the farm and apple orchards when he got his degree. I knew this would be good for him and my father, who is getting older and needs to retire, even though he would never admit it. I knew that if we didn't call the boys on the seventh of September, they would start looking for us. But until then Bo and I were on our own. This was the last week of May, which meant I had a little over three months until I knew someone would be looking for us. So, I needed to find the best place for our permanent camp, but I didn't want it to be too far from the river, or Paul's grave.

Chapter 17

Paul and I camped almost every summer with the boys, so I knew how to set up camp. But here there could be bears, wolves, moose, deer, and who knows what else? I'd already had to deal with the squirrels and magpies. Bo was just about crazy from chasing them, but I knew he was having fun. He just wasn't quite fast enough to catch them. They're both such fast little thieves. I learned quickly that I couldn't leave anything lying out that was shiny! I'd already lost a spoon and my lipstick to one or the other of these pesky little sneak thieves. I wouldn't miss the spoon, but I would really like to have my lipstick back. It was the only one I had brought with me, and I didn't think it was their shade anyway.

I needed to make sure my permanent campsite was where I could defend it if it came to that. I also needed enough trees to disguise the smoke from my fire, just thinking about all that made me a nervous wreck. I just wanted to run and hide. Again, I prayed, "Please God, help me be strong. I have to stay strong."

Come on, Julie, I told myself, *you've put this off long enough.* So, I finished packing my backpack, strapped the pistol around my waist, picked up my rifle, and wrapped Bo's leash around my waist just in case I needed to control him. When all that was done, Bo and I set out on our search. I was hoping to find a cave or an overhang that was big and dry enough to hold the big tent and everything else. I hoped I found something that was easy to get to, easy to defend, and was close to Paul. We must have walked for three miles or more before turning back. The woods were very dense in places, and there were big boulders everywhere. Most of them were too steep to climb, and everything seemed to be covered with moss. It felt as if I was walking on a sponge because the moss was so soft in places. There were some berry patches, not too far in from my present camp, which were in full bloom and would be ready to pick in a few weeks. I've made a rough map of where they are so that I'll be able to come back and pick them when they get ripe. After mapping the berry patches, Bo and I kept looking for the best place to move the camp. I found a beautiful little glen that reminded me of my childhood secret hiding place on the farm. I spent many days there reading, playing, and hiding from my Mother so I wouldn't have to do chores.

I decided this glen was an excellent place to rest, so I took off my jacket and draped it over a huge log that I sat on while Bo and I ate our lunch. I took out my notebook and drew a map of the glen. Then taking the compass out of my pocket, I charted our way back to Paul's grave and our camp.

Paul had made sure that the boys and I knew how to read maps and chart our way back to camp with a compass. He made learning to read the compass, charting, and tracking a game. We played it every time we went camping. Paul would go one way while the boys went their way, and I would go another. We would mark our trails by stacking sticks or stones. We each had a certain amount of sticks or stones to stack. The number of sticks or stones I used was three. I would stack the stones one on top of the other or in the shape of a triangle. Paul's number was five sticks or stones, and he arranged his in a V shape.

When the boys were young, they would try to trick us by using several different numbers and shapes. Sometimes, they would mix sticks and stones together. They never could figure out how Paul and I found them. They never realized that by clearing an area to make their design, or by putting the sticks or stones in some kind of crazy pattern, we would know they had been there. They usually hid somewhere close by to watch and see if they had fooled us. When we came upon their handiwork, Paul and I would make a big show of not noticing it. We would walk around the area listening for their muffled giggles. As soon as we knew where they were, Paul would loudly say, "Well, Julie, I guess the boys haven't been anywhere around here. I guess we'll just have to keep looking. I sure hope they make it back in time for supper." We would walk on and quietly circle around behind them. Sometimes we would just hide and listen to them celebrate tricking us. And other times, we would sneak up on them and scare them. Either way, we always had a lot of fun on those camping trips. It almost makes me wish they were still little boys and we could play our games again.

The boys eventually started taking separate trails and started using their own designs. We all became very good at reading maps and tracking each other. Doing this, we could follow one another, and if someone did not come back when they were supposed to, we would know how to find them. We always had so much fun trying to make our trails as tricky as we could. Not only was it fun, but it was also good training. Now I silently thanked Paul for teaching us how to do this. Maybe he knew someday I would need to know how to do it. I remember him telling us, "You hear so much about people getting lost and dying because they couldn't find their way back to camp. I never want that to happen to any of us."

"Oh Lord," I prayed, "Thank you so much for giving Paul that insight. I would be so much worse off now if I didn't have these skills."

Oh! How I wished Paul could have seen this little glen, he would have loved it. Spring, when things began to come alive and grow, was his favorite time of year. It was so beautiful with the misty green bushes and little yellow and white flowers just peeping out from under cover. I thought this would be a beautiful place for our camp, but I realized that it was too far from the river and Paul's grave. Feeling tears come to my eyes. I told myself to stop it! This was not the time to think of Paul. I must think of keeping myself and Bo alive. I wished I had brought my camera so I could take pictures of the little flowers and the peaceful little glen. I decided I would come back to this place after I had my camp set up, and I would bring the camera with me then.

Chapter 18

Bo had so much fun running in and out exploring the caves. We only found two caves, and they were much too small. The overhangs we found were either too low or too shallow for our use, also. As Bo sat beside me, I talked to him and told him what a brave and good dog he was. It made me feel so much safer having him with me. Because if he hadn't been with me, I would probably still be sitting by Paul's grave crying, not knowing what to do next and being afraid to go any farther. He's such a wonderful guard dog. I knew that he would always let me know if there were any animals or other dangers around.

Dear Diary

June 11
I am so excited! I think I've found the perfect place to put my tent. It is not a cave or an overhang, but four trees spaced almost perfectly apart. There's plenty of space for the big tent inside the trees, and I'll still have enough room between each tree to build walls for a fort, or even a cabin, if I feel that I can build something that big. It's close to a small spring that I

found on one of my earlier scouting trips. It's also far enough away so that no one can see it from the river.

Dear Diary

June 16

It took me almost two days to get the big tent up. It took me half a day just to get the stovepipe up through the top of the tent, but I did it! Now, as I stand here looking at the tent, I think maybe I won't build a fort. I don't really think I would ever be able to dig holes deep enough to hold the poles securely, but perhaps I can build a cabin. There are about two or three feet, on either side of my tent which will give me and Bo room to walk around our tent. I pray that I will have the strength to do this. If nothing else, I can get walls around my tent and a solid door in one of the walls. Just walls and the solid door will give us much more protection than the zipper and flaps of the tent. Just thinking about it makes me giddy with hope. But for now, I need to get everything moved from under the boat and the small tent into the big tent. I will feel so much better when I have everything in one place so I can make sure nothing is getting into it.

Chapter 19

The sun was barely up when I had walked to my lookout. My new campsite was about a half mile farther into the woods than the original one, but the walk was nice. I still felt the need to keep watching for those men, so I spent a part of each morning at the lookout.

My heart almost stopped when I saw them! Thank goodness they were on the other side of the river. I quickly crouched down because I could see that they had binoculars and were scanning both sides of the river. I pulled Bo close to me and told him to be quiet. I held my rifle tightly as I lay watching them, thinking of what might have happened if they had seen me. I trembled as I wondered if I would be able to shoot them if they saw me and came after me. I closed my eyes and prayed that my cover was enough. It had been almost two weeks since I'd heard them planning to rob us and leave us stranded. I thought that perhaps I had missed them and had begun to feel safer. Now, as I watched them, I prayed, "Lord, please let them stay on the other side of the river!" As I watched them drift quietly out of sight, I thought I still must keep up my routine of watching. Bo and I continued to lie and wait for over an hour thinking they might circle back and come down this side of the river. Finally, I decided that it was safe to go back to camp.

Two days had passed since I saw the men on the river, so I thought it would probably be safe to start cutting trees to build the cabin around my tent. And if that worked, I'd try to put on a roof to make it a proper cabin. I'd just have to try because if I could do it, it would be much more secure than just the tent.

It took me two days with a pick and shovel to dig a trench just inside the trees. I knew the trench should be deep enough for two logs, but because of the tree roots and permafrost, one log deep would have to do. I knew I should remove the bark from the logs to keep them from rotting, but I didn't think I had enough time to do that. And I hoped I wouldn't need the cabin past the middle of September, so I wasn't worried about the bark too much. The area where I was going to build my cabin was about ten feet across the front and back and twelve feet on either side. That wouldn't be very big, but it'd do until the boys come to rescue me. That was if I survived building the cabin, or some other calamity.

Seeing the men had almost scared me to death, and I prayed with all my might that they would've just given up and gone back to the outpost. So, I would keep up my routine of going to the lookout for a few more weeks anyway.

Dear Diary

June 16
Today I'll start picking trees to cut. There are some beautiful pine and spruce close by, but I know it'll not be enough to build the cabin. I'm going to use these closer trees first, then move deeper into the forest, as I need to. They are beautiful, tall, straight trees, and it hurts me to cut them, but I'm thankful for them. There doesn't seem to be any oak trees or other hardwoods in this area, but pines and spruce grow straighter and taller anyway, so I don't really need the hardwoods. There should be enough to at least get started on the walls around my tent, so I'll have some protection. I know it won't be easy with just the one-man saw, an ax, and the wedges that I have. I just hope I can hold out. I've never cut a big tree down by myself before. I hope I can remember how to cut the trees so that they'll fall where I want them to. It would completely break me if I cut a tree that fell on my tent or the cabin as I get it up.

Chapter 20

Oh, how Paul and the boys would have laughed at me! The first two trees I cut were bigger than I could possibly pull back to camp even though they weren't far from my tent. Once I had them down and limbed, I couldn't even get them to roll. They wouldn't even budge at all. I was so disgusted with myself. That mistake cost me a full day's work and way too much energy. But I could always cut them for firewood later I decided. So, all that effort wouldn't go to waste. From then on, I knew I had to make sure that the trees were small enough that I could pull them back to camp.

The next day, I cut, topped, and trimmed two smaller trees. Then, I dragged them back to camp. It took me all day to do this, and I was completely exhausted. I knew I couldn't do that every day, so I decided I would cut the trees and get them topped and trimmed on one day and pull them to camp the next. I hoped I could get more trees cut that way. It was exhausting work, and even with gloves my hands were blistered and sore. I don't think there was a part of my body that didn't hurt. How I would've loved to go to bed and stay there for at least a couple of days. But I knew I couldn't. As my father always said, when we would complain about being tired and sore, "You'll just have to work it out. It won't get any better lying around complaining about it."

Over the next five days, I cut trees one day and hauled logs back the next. Then I ran out of trees close to camp that were the size I needed. I was thankful, I hadn't had any mishaps while cutting the trees down. The first few made me nervous, but I soon remembered those childhood lessons on the farm. Each tree had fallen almost exactly where I wanted it to go.

Dear Diary

June 20
Tomorrow, I'll start getting the cabin walls up. This way I'll know approximately how many more trees I'll need to cut. But first I'll make a couple of ladders—one for outside the wall and one for inside the wall. I'm going to make them with trees that are too short, and not big enough around to use for my walls. I'll use some of the limbs that I've trimmed for the rungs. The ladders will need to be at least eight feet tall, and relatively light so I can move them easily. I hope this'll make it easier because I know I can't reach much

higher than four or five feet without them and that won't be high enough to cover the top of the tent.

Building a cabin was much harder than I believed it would be. I guess I thought it would be as easy as it was when I was in my twenties. Paul and I had bought a small farm, which had an old log barn on it that was just about to fall down. Paul decided we should build a new log barn. There was a lot of timber on the place, so we decided to cut the logs off our own land. We spent months cutting, removing the bark, and hauling logs. It took us just about all summer to build that barn which was almost twice as big as my cabin will be. Building that barn was hard work, but we were young and much stronger than I am now. Building the barn was a lot of fun. And, every time we would ride past that farm, after we sold it, it would make us proud to see the barn was still standing.

Getting the walls up was even harder than I thought because it rained every day for almost a week. The rain wasn't hard, just aggravating, and having to wear my bulky rain jacket all the time really slowed me down. It also made the logs slick and hard to manage. The logs weren't all the same size, but I chose four that were closest in size to each other to use in my trench. It took a little trial and error, and they weren't pretty, but I finally managed to get the notches cut in each end of the logs. Then, by pulling and rolling, I managed to get a log in each trench and fitted together. And by using several small rocks, I managed to get them almost level. I also rigged up a pulley system in my anchor trees on each corner. I managed to get a pulley and rope on a high branch in each of these trees. This way, I would be able to tie a rope on each end of the log and lift it into place one end at a time. Thank God Paul thought to bring four pulleys and enough rope for each one. When I asked him why we were bringing so many pulleys, he said there was no way the two of us could lift the logs for the cabin we were going to try to rebuild without them. I know now why he insisted on bringing them. Not only would they make it easier for him *because he had his little secret about his heart*. He also knew that, even with my help, he wouldn't have the strength or stamina to lift those logs without the pulleys.

I knew my progress had been slow, but I was so proud of myself even though my body felt as if I'd been run over by a ten-ton truck. It took me several days, but I managed to get the walls of my cabin three logs high. Well, actually four if you count the ones in the trench. I hoped my body would get used to all this physical labor and the building would go a little faster. That was my prayer every evening as I fell into bed exhausted and sore.

Chapter 21

Dear Diary

June 20
Today is Sunday, and it has been over a week since I've been to Paul's grave. I felt so guilty when I realized it had been that long. Now as I sit here talking to him, telling him my plans for the cabin, I am so very lonely. I just lay my head on Paul's grave and sobbed telling him how much I miss him.

The loneliness was the hardest part, and not having anyone to share things with made me so sad. I don't know how many times I turned to say something to Paul only to be reminded again that he wasn't there. There were so many things I wanted to ask him about. I would go over them in my head every day. I told myself to stop being so foolish because it was a total waste of time. He left me here! And I knew that, somehow, I must survive! Sitting there talking to Paul made me understand why people went to the cemetery every week and sat and talked to their loved ones. I don't think I have ever felt so lost and alone as I did those first few weeks.

I had fallen asleep, but Bo woke me with his growling. He was standing and looking toward the river. The first thing I thought of was rescue! As I got up quickly, I remembered that it might be those men. So, instead of rushing to the river, I took Bo by the collar, and we eased our way to the edge of the woods. I looked through the binoculars and, at first, I saw nothing out of the ordinary. Then looking down the beach, I saw what had caused Bo's growling. A large black bear stood far down the beach by some boulders! He was standing straight up in the water, and he was huge!

I covered my mouth with my hands to keep from screaming and made myself stand still and not run. I was afraid he would hear us. Then I thought, *Oh Lord, what if he smells us?* As I reached down for my rifle, I realized I had left it in camp. I was wearing my pistol, but I knew that it wouldn't do anything to a bear except make it mad. I quietly knelt down beside Bo and wrapped my arm around him. I told him to be very quiet. He was quivering and growling low in his throat, but he stayed still. As we knelt there, the bear turned, looked around, then climbed up over the boulders and disappeared on the other side. I was trembling, as I let out my breath not realizing that I had been holding it. I quietly eased back to Paul's grave.

Whispering, I told him how foolish I felt. What if the bear had come our way? I wouldn't have been able to defend myself or Bo. "Oh Paul," I sobbed quietly. "I can't do this! I can't survive without you! Why did you leave me here all alone?" Finally, with tears in my eyes, I gathered my courage, put Bo on his leash, told Paul goodbye, and ran as fast I could back to camp. Reaching the camp, I grabbed my rifle and hugged it to me, telling Bo I would never go anywhere without it again. Seeing that bear had really terrified me! As I sat there trembling thinking about the bear, I realized how close he was to our camp and that it could be anywhere. As I sat there with one arm around Bo and the other around my gun, I felt scared and foolish. And once again I wished I were home where we would be safe.

That morning really scared me. I was so nervous I couldn't get any work done for thinking about and looking around for the bear. Every little noise I heard made me jump, thinking that it might be the bear. I knew without a shadow of a doubt that I must build the cabin. I finally gave up on getting any work done and fixed supper for myself and Bo. Then, I secured the campsite and went to bed. I was mentally and physically exhausted! I thought I could go to sleep quickly, but I lay awake for what seemed like hours making plans and listening to the night sounds. When I finally fell asleep, I dreamed that the bear was chasing Bo and me. I jumped up wide awake, drenched in sweat, and trembling. I hadn't had a nightmare like that in years. The next morning the dream had left me tired and exhausted. How I wished I could stay in bed. But I knew that I had work to do, and I couldn't afford the luxury of a day off. So, I got up, got dressed, and fixed myself toast and coffee. I fed Bo, and when we had eaten, I went to work.

Chapter 22

I worked two weeks, and by using the pulleys and ropes, I managed to get a total of five logs up on each side of my cabin which made the walls just a little over four feet tall. It took me longer than I expected, but I also had to cut out the opening for my door. When I started this, I realized I needed to block up each of the short logs to keep them level until I got the door frame in place. Cutting and placing the blocks, was as confusing as putting together an elaborate jigsaw puzzle.

After I had the blocks in place, and everything was stable, I decided to take a break from stacking the walls to split some logs to use for the door frame and header. It took me all of one day to plane and smooth them. I knew I was getting ahead of myself, but I couldn't wait to get my door in place. With my brace and bit, I planned to drill holes into the frame and the logs of the walls. When the boards were done, I planned to fasten them with pegs instead of nails. I decided to use some of the smaller branches for the pegs. There were plenty of them, and they wouldn't require much work to shape them to the right size.

It was backbreaking work, but it was still easier than putting up logs. And, it gave my body a little rest. I knew I needed to get at least four more logs up before my walls would be high enough to put the door frame and header in place, but I'd have them ready.

Dear Diary

June 23
I'm pleased with the outcome so far. I'll feel so much safer with the door in place. I can hardly wait. Just to have a door that I can close makes me so excited. Oh, how I wish Paul could see my work. I know he would be so proud of me. Tomorrow I'll start on my door. It'll be a little less than six foot tall, but that'll be tall enough for me. I've decided to use the trees I first cut down. They are really close to my cabin so I can take the ax and wedges over and see if I can get them to split somewhat evenly. If this works, I should be able to get four or five planks from each tree. I shouldn't need that many for the door itself, but the extra planks can be used to make the braces.

Dear Diary

June 23

I've run out of logs, and I'll have to go farther into the woods to find more trees that are the right size. But, before I do that, I'm going to get my door installed. I've got my brace and bit ready, I've made the pegs, and I'm ready to start drilling. I'm going to try setting the frame in the opening so I can drill through it and the logs at the same time. That way the holes will match up. I hope the frame fits tightly enough for this. It will if I measured it right. I made hinges for the door out of a pair of Paul's boots, and I hope they'll work. I decided to make a drop bar latch. It'll have a rope attached so that I can drop a bar into a hook. The bar will pivot on a wooden peg, and the hook will also be made from wood. The rope on the bar will be on the opposite end from the peg and will pass through a hole in the door. This way the door will be secure from the inside and the outside, and I can't lock myself out. At night, I will be able to pull the rope inside and wrap it around a bent nail. This lock may not stop people, but it should keep the animals out. I can't wait to get everything put together. It'll probably take me all day, but I'm going to have my door in place before I go to bed!

I worked way into the night, but the door is in. I think it's beautiful and I feel very secure just looking at it.

The next morning, I started my search for a new place to cut logs. I finally found a place, about a mile from camp, with trees that are the right size. It took most of the day to find the spot, so I decided to start cutting the next day. I was going to try to cut and limb two trees each day. Then I'd pull them back to camp in the evening.

My plan didn't work. I didn't have any trouble getting two logs ready to take back with me, but when I attached them to the rope harness I'd made, I found out I couldn't pull both of them back at the same time. When I tried to pull the two logs, I could barely move them. I just didn't have the strength. So, my new plan was to cut and limb three trees each day but only pull one back with me at night. I was worried that at that rate, it might take me weeks to finish the cabin. It also made me nervous being that far from camp, but I knew it had to be done, and staying busy kept me from hiding in the tent feeling sorry for myself.

Chapter 23

Dear Diary

July 1
It's Sunday, and I've decided to stay close to camp and do chores. I need to wash clothes, bathe, and haul drinking water from the spring. Taking my guns and my sled, I head to the river.

I made the sled earlier by using some short logs that I couldn't use for the cabin. I split them into planks and put runners on the bottom like a bobsled. I made side rails to keep things from falling off and attached a rope harness to pull it with. It's so much easier carrying things from place to place with the sled than having to carry them in my arms. I'm quite proud of my handiwork. It looks good, and so far, it works well.

I gathered my buckets and dirty laundry along with a change of clean clothes and put them on the sled, and then Bo and I headed for the small inlet on the river. I found the inlet soon after Paul's death while I was exploring for a permanent campsite. As I reached the water, I took my binoculars and made sure to scan the area for those horrible men or any large animals that might be around. Then I took off my dirty clothes, gathered up the rest of my dirty things, and waded into the water. I had found that this was the best way to wash. After washing and rinsing all my clothes, I carried them back to the sled putting them in one of the buckets. Then I waded back into the water to bathe myself and wash my hair. The water felt so good I didn't want to get out, so I just lay back in the water, floating and watching the clouds. I floated there completely content until Bo decided it was time for me to play fetch with him. We played for a while. I would throw the stick out as far I could, and he would swim out, retrieve it, and then bring it back to me. I threw the stick until I was good and tired. On the last throw, Bo brought the stick back, but when he dropped it, he started growling and swimming for shore.

My heart nearly stopped because I knew we were not alone! I slowly turned, half expecting to see the men standing there! I was afraid they might have come back! Instead, there stood a half-grown moose! He must have come around the boulders without making a sound! And now there he stood chewing on my wet clothes! He had turned over my sled and dumped out my bucket of clean clothes. And here I was in the waist deep water as naked as the day I was born! Not knowing what else to do I started easing toward the shore. Bo was already on the beach. He was between me and the moose, standing his ground, growling deep in his throat. As I climbed out of the water, Bo started to bark. I jumped like I was shot! I don't know who was more startled, the moose or me. I don't think I had ever heard Bo bark that much, or that loud! He very seldom barked at anything. The moose just stood there watching us trying to figure out what we were. I was afraid Bo would run at the moose, or the moose might charge him, but Bo just stood there barking. I tried to stop him, but he just barked louder. The moose just stood there chewing on my clothes and watching us for a few more minutes. Then dropping my chewed-up shirt, he turned, silently walked back around the boulder, and ambled into the woods.

I quickly grabbed my towel and wrapped it around me. I sat down beside Bo hugging him and telling him how brave he was. As I sat there wrapped in my towel, holding my rifle, I began to cry. Oh, how I wished I were back in Seattle where things were safe and secure. I asked God again, "Why did you let us come to Alaska? WHY?" I couldn't help thinking that if we had stayed home, Paul would still be alive! I wouldn't be stranded here wrapped only in a towel trying to survive! Bo wouldn't have to protect me from wild animals, and killer men! And my favorite shirt wouldn't have just been eaten by a moose!

As I sat there trembling and praying, suddenly I was laughing uncontrollably. Just the thought of that poor little moose and wondering what in the world he must be thinking, had me laughing so hard I was crying. I just sat there laughing with Bo jumping and running all around me. When I could finally control myself, I dropped my towel, gathered up my clothes, waded back into the water, and rinsed them again. Then I waded out of the water, got dressed, gathered everything on the sled, and headed back to camp.

On our way back to camp, I went by the little spring that I had found the first week I was here. What a Godsend it was. It made life so much easier. Before I found it, I had to boil river water at least twice a day. The spring was so pretty. It bubbled up from the ground and ran over some rocks and fell into a deep rock basin. It was just perfect. After cleaning out the debris, the water was clean and very cold. I filled my other two buckets with drinking water and headed home. It was late when we reached camp. I felt rested and at peace. Seeing the moose made me realize that not everything here was out to get me.

After hanging my clothes to dry on a makeshift clothesline, I just sat and thanked God for keeping us safe. I still laugh when I think about that moose. I think it'll be a scene that I'll never forget. I wish I had taken the camera to the inlet with me. The boys would have gotten such a laugh out of seeing the moose chewing my shirt to shreds. The first few weeks I was here, I always had the camera with me. I took pictures of everything I thought might be important or of interest to the boys just in case something happened to me, too. Now, I only used it to record the progress on the cabin because my supply of film was running low. I sat for the longest time just watching the sky. It was so beautiful. I felt as if I could reach up and touch the stars. How could I feel so peaceful here one minute and scared to death the next?

Dear Diary

July 2
I've got to gather my thoughts and try to make plans for cutting more logs next week. I get so lost in daydreams on a day like today, but I know I have to keep planning and working on surviving this

ordeal. I think I'll try to cut at least three trees a day like I have been doing. I only need about three or four more logs on all sides, and if my strength holds out, I'll have my walls finished soon. I can only bring one tree back to camp each day, so that's what's going to slow me down. Maybe I'll cut and prepare the logs for three or four days, then take a day just to pull logs back to camp. I might be able to get four or five logs to the cabin in one day. I'm not sure if I can make that many round trips in one day, but I'm going to try. If I do it this way, it will give my arms a rest. They are so sore now that I can barely cook us a meal at the end of the day. I hope that I can pull the logs up as high as they'll need to go. I know I could never have gotten this far without the pulleys; thank you, Paul, for bringing them. Once I get the walls up then comes the roof. I don't know quite how I'll do that, but I'll get it done somehow.

Oh, I can't keep my mind on plans right now. The sky is much too beautiful tonight, and I feel so at peace with the world. I know that soon I'll have to go inside. It'll soon be time for bed, and I still need to feed Bo and eat something myself.

I try to be in bed by 9 o'clock which seems so weird when it's still light outside, but I know if I don't get at least seven or eight hours of sleep I won't have the strength to continue working on the cabin.

Over the next week, I concentrated on getting enough logs cut and hauled to the cabin. I finally had a good pile of logs at the cabin ready to stack. I moved the pulleys higher into the trees, so I would have plenty of room to get the logs in place. The next day was Sunday, and Bo and I always took that day off. I needed to do laundry and bathe. The water always eased the aches in my muscles. I also really needed to visit Paul's grave. I had so much to tell him. Visiting his grave had become part of our Sunday routine. Sunday had always been our day of worship and rest, so I spent as much of the day with him as I could.

It took longer than I thought it would, but I was able to place at least one log on each wall every day, and my walls are finally done. The walls are just two logs taller than the door so that makes them close to seven and a half feet tall. I would've liked them to be at least eight feet tall, but my strength was gone so they'd have to be tall enough. They cleared the top of the tent, and that's really all the height I needed. Even though

I'd built up a lot more muscle, my strength was just about gone, and I had to reserve something for the job of getting a roof on the cabin. I was proud of my work, and I remember thinking the boys would surely get a kick out of my handiwork. As I had done with each milestone in building the cabin, I took out my camera and took a picture to record my progress.

Chapter 24

I decided to take some time to clean up around the camp. I also wanted to make some bread. We were getting tired of flapjacks. Well, at least I was. Bo would eat anything. I knew we needed to eat more than beans, beef hash, dried apples, and flapjacks. I really needed to take a day to go foraging for fresh greens, other edible vegetables, and berries.

After I had set the bread to rise, I decided I would take my buckets and go to the river. Since I'd have around an hour before the bread would be ready to bake, I decided I might even explore along one of the little creeks, that I'd not had time to explore yet, just to see what I could find. So, I got my rifle, the buckets, a few empty bags loaded on the sled, and Bo and I went foraging.

The first thing we found was a beautiful patch of wild roses in full bloom. I thought that this would be a good thing when winter came. I could come back and get a good supply of rosehips to make rosehip jelly if I could spare the sugar. They're also good for making cold tonics and for a lot of other medicinal things. But now wasn't the time for them to be picked, and I really hoped, deep down inside, that I wouldn't be here in the winter to collect any of them.

As Bo and I walked up and down the little stream, we found a lot of herbs and vegetables that I knew were edible. We found watercress, chickweed, and some fiddlehead ferns and a plant that looked almost like a wild onion but smelled like garlic. I gathered them thinking maybe the onions would be great in soups and some of the rest would make an excellent salad, but the fiddleheads I knew would be delicious just cooked in a little lard. With my bags full, I started back to camp thinking my bread would be ready to put in the oven by the time we got back. That day was just what I had needed. I felt quite rested and satisfied with our finds.

Chapter 25

I cut, topped, and trimmed four trees for the roof, and I pulled one log back with me each day. I was genuinely exhausted, but happy. I decided to split each log; that should make it much easier to get them up on the roof. I also decided that I would slant the roof like a lean-to. That way the rain or snow would run off the back, and the roof would be less likely to leak. I knew I'd have to put one more log on the front of the cabin, and I really wasn't looking forward to it, but I really felt that would be the best way for me to get a roof on the cabin. I sure hoped that it would work. It had taken me almost two months just to get this far, and that was working almost every day. I was so ready to be finished with the cabin. I wanted to cry just thinking about having to add that one extra log to the front, not to mention getting a roof on it.

I had made two trips to my work site, and I was headed back to the cabin when Bo began to growl deep in his throat. I grabbed him and pulled him close to me just as he started to run. Holding him by the collar, I told him, "NO BO NO"! He was so upset he almost pulled me down before I could fasten the leash to his collar. I clumsily unfastened the rope harness from around my waist with one hand while holding the leash in the other. I needed to be free of the log just in case I had to run.

I kept telling Bo to be quiet, but he paid me no attention. He was fighting mad, and he wasn't going to quit until he could get whatever it was. I knew it must be a big animal, and I was as scared as Bo was mad. "Please, God, just let it be a moose, not a bear or a wolf," I prayed. I just stood still looking around and listening for a few minutes but not seeing anything unusual. Not knowing what to expect, I checked my guns, making sure they were ready to fire. I quickly tied Bo's leash to my belt so I could have both hands free if I needed to use the rifle. As we rounded the next boulder, Bo went crazy, jumping, pulling, trying with all his might to get loose. But I pulled him closer to me and took hold of his collar.

As I looked up, I froze. There on the boulder sat a huge black bear! He was just sitting there looking down at us, as if to say, "I could have had you anytime I wanted." It was all I could do not to run. Holding Bo, I crouched there, trying not to look directly at the bear. I thanked God again that Bo was not a barking dog. He was so mad he was trembling, growling viciously, and lunging, trying to get free! I kept begging him to "please be quiet" that everything would be okay, but to no avail. All he wanted was to take care of that bear. It took all my strength to hold him and try not to drop the rifle.

After several minutes of just looking at the bear, I knew what had to be done. There was no other path to the cabin so we would have to follow this trail and pass directly under where he sat. I was terrified! I slowly stood up. I only let Bo have enough leash to keep him right beside me. He tried and tried to pull out of my grasp, but I wasn't going to let him go for anything. Finally, I got up the courage to take that first step. I could feel the bear watching us every step we took. As I slowly walked on, dragging a very furious Bo with me, the bear continued to just sit there. I walked as slowly as possible, dragging Bo, and glancing back occasionally to make sure the bear wasn't following us. It took all the strength and courage I could muster.

The minute I knew the bear couldn't see us I broke and ran, dragging Bo with me!

Reaching camp, and with shaking hands, I opened the door and dragged Bo inside as I frantically pulled the string in and locked it behind us. I stumbled into the tent, fell to the floor, and scooted back against the bed. Pulling Bo to me, I held him as tightly as I could without hurting him. I was trembling uncontrollably, and so was Bo. The difference was that I was trembling with fear, and Bo was trembling with anger. He had wanted that bear and was furious at me for not letting him have it!

I don't think I've ever been so afraid in my life. I felt as if I couldn't breathe, and thought I was having a heart attack. My heart was beating so hard it felt as if it would jump out of my chest at any minute. I put my head between my knees to keep from passing out, as nausea kept washing over me. "Dear, Lord, please help me!" I pleaded. "I want to go home!" I screamed over and over. I hid my face in Bo's fur as I sat there shaking and crying. I was angry at myself for being so weak, angry at Paul for leaving us here, angry at the bear for being on MY trail, angry at Bo for being angry at me, and angry at God for allowing all of this to happen!

Bo was still mad. He kept growling and grumbling at me, but I just didn't care. I kept telling him what a good and brave dog he was. I tried to explain that the bear would have killed him if he had run after it. But it didn't make any difference to him. He was still mad, and he still wanted that bear. I tried to stand, but my legs just wouldn't hold me up. So, I slid back down to the floor. I hugged my knees up to my chest to help control the trembling. I told myself that I had to get over this. I had things to do, and I couldn't hide in the cabin forever.

Chapter 26

Dear Diary

July 12
My walls will be truly finished when I get the log across the front so my roof will slant. Then I can start laying the rafters on. Before I get started, I'll have to move the pulleys at the front of the cabin, to a higher spot. Using the pulleys and the ladders, I should be able to get each rafter in place without much trouble. I'll notch the ends of the rafters before I pull them up, and then slide them into place. I'll have to move the ladders several times and make a lot of trips up and down the steps, but I think I can get it done relatively quickly. I have the log for the front and eight rafters already split and ready to be put on the roof. I used logs that were smaller in diameter than the ones I used for the walls because these rafters will have to be at least sixteen feet long so I will have an adequate overhang. Tomorrow I'll move the front pulleys and get that last log up. Then, I'll try to get

these rafters on the cabin. After I use all the logs I have in camp, I'll be able to get a more accurate count of how many more I'll need to completely finish the roof.

With the help of the pulleys and ladders, I managed to get some of the rafters on the roof. Cutting the notches before I pulled the rafters up was very helpful. I'd gotten pretty good at cutting notches, and although I had to modify them sometimes after I got them on the roof, they helped to keep the rafter from sliding off the backside of the cabin while I was working it into place.

Dear Diary

July 15
The mosquitoes are just terrible! Even with a mosquito net at night I still can't rest for their buzzing. Although I rub my face and neck and any other exposed skin with mud during the day, they still find a way to bite. I even tried wetting a couple of old shirts, rolling them into tight balls, and putting them on the edge of the fire, so they will smoke to help drive the mosquitoes away, but it only helps when I can stand in the smoke. Poor little Bo just rolls in the grass

and scratches himself; they are driving him crazy. For the last few nights, I've made him sleep on the bed with me under the mosquito netting. He doesn't like the bed. He had much rather sleep on the floor. But it's better than the mosquitoes biting him, and we both got a little more sleep. I have tried rubbing mud in his ears and all over his face and belly, but he just rolls and rubs it off, so I decided it wasn't worth the effort.

It had been four days since we saw the bear. I had used all the logs that I'd pulled into camp and knew that I had to go get the ones that I had cut, bear or no bear. I packed my backpack and made sure I had both my pistol and rifle loaded. Then putting the leash on Bo, we started back into the forest. Bo was not happy being on the leash. But, until I knew it was safe for him, he'd have to stay on the leash. He'd just have to deal with it until we got to the logs and I knew the bear was nowhere around. I certainly hoped it was long gone, because if it wasn't, I'd have to kill it. And I didn't have the time to deal with cleaning a bear just then. I had to finish the roof and chink the walls to finish my cabin.

I was stiff with fear and jumped at every rustle in the bushes. When we finally came to the place where we had seen the bear, I breathed a sigh of relief. He was not there. Then, as I continued down the path, I saw my rope harness and the log right where I had dropped them. As I fastened the harness around my waist, I giggled to myself. I thought it had surely taken me a lot longer to get here today than it did to get to the cabin when I thought I had a bear chasing me.

I could tell by the way Bo was acting that the bear was long gone. I was so relieved! With a sigh of relief, I let Bo off his leash. He was much happier, and so was I. It seemed that the bear had moved on to another area.

Because most of the tools were at the work site, I decided to split the four logs there that I had cut earlier before dragging them back to the cabin. I hoped I could pull two halves at a time, as easily as I could pull one whole log. I'd still have to make four trips, and I hoped my strength would hold out. If it did, I should be able to make all the trips in one day. At least I was going to try. I was pretty sure those logs would finish my roof, and if they did, I knew I would shout with joy!

I prayed that those split logs would be enough to finish the roof. When I finished getting this layer on, I planned to spread my large tarp over them, and then anchor it down with smaller poles. If the tarp wasn't large enough to cover the entire roof, I was going to use the small tent to fill in the space. I knew I might have to take it apart, but I wanted the cabin to be as waterproof as possible, so I didn't mind sacrificing the small tent.

I still had to cut the smaller poles to place in between each of the larger split logs. By nailing them into place, they should hold the tarp secure and make the roof as solid as it could be. Thank goodness, there were smaller trees growing closer to the cabin, and I wouldn't have to go so far into the woods to get them.

By late afternoon, I had gotten much more done than I thought I would. I'd gotten all four logs split and ready to drag. I modified my harness by changing the pull rope from one spot in the back to a rope on each side. This way, I could pull two split logs at the same time. After cleaning up the area, I packed up all my gear and got ready to go. I practiced pulling the logs around camp for a little while just to get used to the way they would drag and shift their weight. I was so relieved to see that with practice I could pull them as easily as I pulled one single log.

Keeping the harness on, I called Bo to come to me. I had to put him back on the leash even though I knew he would hate it. *Well*, I thought, *he'll just have to hate it. Right now, I can't handle the trips up and down the trail being scared that he's going to take off after some animal.* After I got Bo hooked up, I picked up my backpack, and we started back to camp. I kept watching the boulders. Even though we had cleared quite a good trail back to camp, there were still boulders that I couldn't see around, and it made me nervous. I kept thinking, what if the bear is just around the next corner? I kept watching Bo for any sign that something was wrong. Thank the Lord, nothing happened, and I was extremely relieved when I finally saw the cabin up ahead.

Chapter 27

But…my relief was short-lived. On my final trip back to camp, with the last logs, I knew right away that something was wrong because every hair on Bo's back was standing on end and he was growling fiercely. He charged around the cabin pulling me, logs, and all with him. When I finally got control of him, I quickly stepped out of the rope harness letting the logs fall to the ground. I grabbed Bo's leash and pulled him close to me, then I drew my pistol. Holding Bo by the collar, and with the pistol ready, we eased around the corner of the cabin. Bo was growling and grumbling and sniffing the air. Looking down I saw the paw prints. At first, I thought they were wolf's prints. They look almost like a dog's track, but they were too wide and had five toes. When I looked closer, I knew it couldn't be a wolf because this thing had claws that were much longer than dogs or wolves would be. I could see where it had tried to dig under the log wall but hadn't been able to, even though he had dug in quite a few places. *I think it's a wolverine!* I just stood there praying, "Oh, Lord, don't let him be inside the wall!" I didn't know much about wolverines. Did wolverines even climb? If they did, could they climb high enough to go over the wall? Oh, Lord! What was I supposed to do if it was inside?

Paul had told me a little about wolverines. He said they are very vicious, mean little critters that could crush bones with their teeth like they were nothing and could move as fast as lightning. He also told me if I were to come in contact with one, I should shoot first and asked questions later. They had been known to take down animals much larger than they were. One of them could rip Bo or me to shreds in a matter of minutes. Why, oh why, didn't I study up on the animals in Alaska? Especially the ones that could kill us!

I dragged Bo to the door and quietly opened it, praying that the wolverine was not waiting on the other side. As I stepped inside, I started to close the door behind me but decided I had better leave it open just in case the wolverine or whatever it might be was inside. I eased the rifle and backpack off my shoulders while still holding Bo's leash because I wanted to have as much ability to move as possible. Also, if I did have to run, I didn't want anything to slow me down.

I kept the pistol tightly gripped in my right hand. I hoped it would be powerful enough to kill whatever animal might be in the cabin. I couldn't let Bo go, and I couldn't control the rifle one-handed so the pistol would have to work. When I saw that Bo wasn't trying to rush inside but kept trying to run back around the cabin to find the wolverine if that's what it was, I knew that it wasn't inside. Keeping my pistol ready, I pulled Bo inside, picked up my rifle, closed the door, and pulled the rope inside to secure it. I kept telling Bo that that thing was meaner and bigger than he was and would kill him. I tried to comfort him, as I removed his leash, but he wouldn't listen to me. Instead, he kept lunging at the door trying to get out.

I just stood there with my back against the wall with tears running down my face. I had been a nervous wreck all day watching for the bear. Then, getting back to the cabin and finding that what I thought was a wolverine had paid us a visit was just more than my nerves could take! I just stood there taking deep breaths trying to calm down and trying to calm Bo and stop him from trying to dig out. He just couldn't understand why I wouldn't let him go after that creature.

I slowly slid down the wall and sat on the ground and cried. I kept telling myself, "Stop crying! It will do no good! You have to get tough!" All at once I was shouting and shaking my fists at the heavens. "This is my cabin! Damn it!" I shouted, "and by God, you can't have it! Do you hear me? Do you hear me?" Then in an exhausted whisper, I said, "When I'm rescued, you can do whatever you damn well please with it! But until then it's mine!" I covered my face with my hands, leaned my head back against the wall, and closed my eyes. I don't know how, but I immediately fell asleep. When I woke up, I was lying curled up in the fetal position, on the ground with Bo lying curled beside me. His head was propped on my side like he had been trying to comfort me. As I hugged him to me, he whined and washed my face. As I lay there, I raised my face to the heavens and with a sigh of resignation, I asked, "What next, Lord?" What next?"

Chapter 28

Early the next day, I got the answer to the question of what animal had visited us yesterday. I was on the ladder inside the walls trying to get another rafter across the roof when I saw a wolverine at the edge of the woods. He was just sitting there watching. Bo must have smelled him at about the same time that I saw him because he was absolutely going crazy. Growling viciously, he ran to the door jumping against it. Thank goodness, I had closed the door! He was so mad. He was trying his best to get out! He wanted to get to that wolverine! Hurrying down the ladder for my gun I slipped and twisted my ankle. It hurt so bad I thought I was going to pass out! "Oh, Lord please don't let my ankle be broken," I cried. "It just can't be broken!"

Poor little Bo didn't know what to do. He wanted to get the wolverine, but he also wanted to make sure I was okay. He kept running to the door growling and scratching to get out and then back to me whining and licking my face. As I sat rubbing my ankle, I tried to assure him I was okay. Finally, I had to hold him to make him quit trying to dig under the wall. This didn't make him any happier, but he would just have to be mad. I couldn't get up, and I couldn't stand the thought of him digging out and going after the wolverine.

Chapter 29

I couldn't work on the cabin for over a week. For two or three days I just sat with my foot propped up rubbing it with liniment and keeping it wrapped tightly. I was aggravated with myself and so angry at that wolverine, I could have screamed!

Dear Diary

July 20
I've managed to hobble around, with the use of a crutch I made doing what was necessary, but not much more. I've been cooped up inside for eight days, but I'm almost out of water, so I'm going to have to go to the spring. I spent a good amount of time this morning trying to decide how I'll be able to do this, and I've finally come up with a plan that I think will work. I plan on putting the buckets on the sled instead of carrying them like I've done in the past. Then, I'll attach the sled to my rope harness. This way, I'll be able to use the crutch and hold Bo's leash with the other hand. I'll have my pistol, and I'll kill that wolverine if it should show up. I know it'll

be slow going, but it must be done, and this is the best plan I can come up with.

As we hobbled and hopped our way to the spring, I kept talking to Bo. I knew he didn't understand that the leash was for his own good. As we got to the spring and I started to dip one of the buckets into the water, I got a glimpse of myself. I gasped and jumped back, dropping my bucket, and almost dragging Bo and the sled into the water. I didn't recognize myself. I looked like an old hag. For just a moment I thought someone else was there. But, at the same time, I knew it was me. Looking at myself again, I wondered how long it had been since I'd brushed my hair. Staring at my reflection in the water I didn't know whether to laugh or cry. I just stood there staring at my reflection thinking to myself, *Julie, you're a mess,* as tears ran down my face.

I quickly retrieved my bucket and filled it and the other one. I put the buckets back on the sled, and then Bo and I hobbled our way back to the cabin. Praise the Lord we didn't run into any animals along the way.

I took one of the buckets and poured water into my washbasin. Then I washed my face and brushed my hair vigorously pulling it back and fastening it at the nape of my neck. I was angry at myself for having no more pride in how I looked. Looking in the camp mirror, I wished I could erase the lines and wrinkles from my face as easily as I fixed my hair. I searched through my bag and found my face cream and applied it quite heavily. I gave myself a good talking to, that from now on I'd take more care in how I looked, even if I was here by myself! Even though I hadn't been able to put weight on my ankle was no excuse for not brushing my hair and washing my face!

Dear Diary

July 21
It's been three days since our trip to the spring, and Bo is very miserable because I'll only let him out of the tent to run around the inside wall of the cabin. He just lies on the floor watching me and pouting, he is so exasperated with me, and with this whole situation. I'm beginning to worry about him. He's almost stopped eating. He just walks round and round the wall growling under his breath. Just listening and waiting for the wolverine, which has paid us a visit almost, every day. It keeps trying to dig under the wall, which sends Bo into a frenzy of growling and grumbling. I have to keep him inside the

tent when the wolverine's here because, if he's outside the tent, as the wolverine tries to dig under the wall from the outside, Bo angrily growls and tries to dig out from the inside, until it has just about driven me crazy. No matter how much I scold him, he just won't listen to me. I've made up my mind. Tomorrow if that little beast, shows up I will somehow climb the ladder no matter how much it hurts, and kill him. I hate to kill him because he's such a beautiful animal, but he's kept us prisoners long enough. It's come down to either him or us, so he'll have to die!

Chapter 30

The day after I finally had to kill the wolverine, I managed to hobble to Paul's grave. Bo was disgusted with me because I had to put him on the leash. Even though the wolverine was dead, I just couldn't let him run free yet. Between the bear and the wolverine, I was still too uneasy. I knew he didn't like it, but he'd just have to pout for a few more days at least. When we got there, Bo calmed down and quietly laid his head on Paul's grave. He looked so sad. I burst into tears because I knew he was missing Paul as much as I was. I sat and began to tell Paul all the things that had happened and what a nervous wreck I was.

"Oh, Paul, these last few weeks have just about finished me," I moaned. "I need you, Paul! I need your strength! I need your knowledge! But, most of all, I just need you! I need you right here beside me! I need your arms wrapped around my shoulders! I need to be able to lean into you and cry until I can't cry anymore! Oh, how I need you!

"You won't believe all that's happened these last few weeks. First of all, one day, as I was coming back from cutting logs, there was a bear sitting on a boulder. He was just sitting there watching us, but it almost scared me to death. I dropped the logs and somehow managed to catch hold of Bo's collar. It was all I could do to keep him from running after it. You wouldn't believe the growls that came out of our little dog. He sounded more vicious than a wolf. When we were out of sight of the bear, I ran for my life! Literally! I was dragging Bo and running as hard as I've ever run. I went straight back to the cabin and locked us in. Four days later, when I finally got up the nerve, I went back to retrieve my logs. I was so scared and nervous, I was so afraid the bear would still be there, but he wasn't, thank God. It took four trips to get all my logs back to camp.

"On the last trip back to the cabin, a wolverine had been there and had tried to dig under the wall. Of course, I didn't know it was a wolverine until the next day. I just knew it was a wolf that had tried to get into the cabin, and I was scared to death that it would come back. It did come back the next day, and that's when I saw what it was. I was up on the ladder inside the cabin working when I saw it. As I hurried down the ladder to get the gun, so I could scare it away or kill it, I slipped and twisted my ankle. I haven't been able to work on the cabin since then or do much of anything else. That wolverine came back every single day.

"You would have respected that hateful little critter because he had so much determination. He kept Bo and me prisoners for over a week until I finally had to go get water. Oh, Paul, you would have been so ashamed of me! While I was getting the water, I got a glimpse of myself. I looked like one of those homeless bag ladies that live on the far side of town. I promised God, right then and there, that if He allowed me to be rescued, I'd make sure to help as many of those poor women as I could. I've made so many promises to God, I really hope I can deliver on them all. I've been writing them down in my diary so I can remember them, and so that I won't be so tempted to forget them when I get home.

"Yesterday, I'd finally had all that I could take of the wolverine. Even though it hurt both physically and emotionally, I was able to climb the ladder and kill him. I didn't want to kill him, but he didn't leave me any other choice. I tried to scare it away, first. I tried everything I could think of. I yelled at him, I threw rocks and wood blocks at him, I even shot over his head, but he just sat there watching us. Then, he'd go right back to trying to dig under the wall. So, with tears in my eyes, I finally took aim and shot him.

"I don't know how much longer I can do this, Paul! I need you to help me! Oh, Paul," I sobbed! At some point in my conversation with Paul, Bo had come over and laid his head in my lap. Now, as I sat there telling Paul about the wolverine and all my woes, he snuggled into my chest and whimpered. I knew then that he'd finally forgiven me for the last few weeks. As I sat there rubbing Bo behind the ears, I could almost hear Paul laughing at me. "Don't be such a baby. You're my brave Julie girl. You know you just did what you had to do."

"You wouldn't believe how long the claws on that thing were, Paul. After I'd killed it and gone out to take care of the carcass, I realized that it wasn't much bigger than Bo. But goodness, his teeth and claws were deadly. He would've been able to rip Bo or me to shreds if he'd have gotten the chance. I took some pictures for my records. I've done this with almost all the new things that happened since I've been here. I hope the pictures turn out good. I know the boys will love seeing the wolverine. Maybe then they'll realize their mom's tougher than they thought she was." I continued talking to Paul and just told him all I could think of.

"I started to just bury the thing or throw it in the river," I said, "but I decided to clean it. I kept the hide and gave Bo some of the meat. Lord, it smelled awful, but Bo thought it was delicious. I took some boards, nailed them together, and stretched the skin on it to dry like we had done with those raccoon hides years ago, remember, Paul? But Bo kept trying to tear it off the boards, until I finally had to take it and nail it high up in a tree where he couldn't reach it." I imagined that Paul was laughing with me on these adventures. I still didn't know what I'd do with the fur, but maybe I'd be able to use it for something.

"I know if anyone should see or hear me, they would think I'd lost my mind. Sitting here bawling like a baby and talking to a grave, but it helps me so much just to talk to you, Paul. I know you can't hear me, but it helps me just the same to tell you what I've been doing, and everything that's happened. Just to be able to tell you what I've gotten done on the cabin, and the scares I got from the bear and the wolverine helps me so much. Just talking things out helps to reassure me that I've done the right thing and it keeps me from feeling so lonesome and all alone. Oh, Paul, I miss you so much!"

"Paul did you know the 4th of July just slip by without me even noticing it. Even though we knew we wouldn't be home for the celebrations this year, I'm miserable. It wouldn't be so bad if you were here with me, but the memories and the sadness are driving me crazy. All the relatives and friends would have been together and catching up on all the gossip and family news. Oh, how I miss that! We missed the games and the excitement and the pie eating contest. I remember the year Todd won that contest. Goodness, he was one sick little boy. He was so ill he couldn't even play ball with his team that evening. It breaks my heart to think that I might never get to attend this celebration again. Paul and the boys always went ahead to get signed up for the ball games, which were the main event of the holiday, because it gave the winning team bragging rights for the entire year. I stayed home fixing the lunch and came to the park later in the day. There always had to be potato salad, fried chicken, and all the trimmings. We also had to have lemonade and homemade vanilla ice cream. I cooked for days making Paul's favorite apple pies. I also made chocolate cake, which was Todd's favorite. Joey always said everything was his favorite. That way he didn't have to limit himself to one dessert; he could have some of it all. Just thinking about it was making me hungry. I especially missed the lemonade. I could almost taste it now.

I wondered if the boys went to the park for the Fourth of July celebration this year. And I wondered if Amy signed up to play ball with Todd on the couple's team like she did last year. Or, if she stayed home to fix the picnic lunch since I'm not there? They were so cute together at the game last year. They spent so much time flirting, their teammates finally told them to stop it or leave the field because they were going to cost them the game. They chose to leave, and we didn't see them again until the fireworks show that night. I wish I had gotten to know her better before we left for Alaska. I hope they're happy. I wonder if Joey brought his girlfriend. I wonder if he has a girlfriend. Oh, how I wish I could have been there! It was so hard not knowing what our boys were doing. I wondered if they missed us. I wondered if they could feel that something was wrong.

I could always tell when something was wrong with Paul or the boys, even if he didn't say anything to me about it. *Oh Lord, why, didn't I know something was wrong with Paul this time?* I thought. *I've always been able to tell when something was wrong. Was I so caught up with my own things, like Todd's wedding and all the festivities, that I left him out? Oh, how could I have gotten so busy that I didn't pay him any attention?* And then I felt myself deflate, thinking, *is that why I didn't know about his heart? Oh, Paul, please forgive me!* I thought, miserably. *I love you so much! If I had paid more attention, maybe you would still be alive. Oh, God how can I live with these thoughts!*

Sometimes I'm so lonesome I feel as if I could just lie down on Paul's grave and die, then I get angry with myself thinking how selfish I'm being! Please, God, help me to stay positive! "Oh, Stop It!" I told myself. "You can't feel sorry for yourself and do the things that you to must do to survive, until the boys come to rescue you." *Oh, Lord! How many times have I played that rescue scene over and over in my head?* I thought. "I know it won't make that day come any quicker, but I can't help dwelling on it sometimes. I know I have to leave it in your hands, and it's my job to stay alive, but that doesn't keep me from daydreaming about it."

Chapter 31

When I left Paul's grave, I decided to go to our inlet and take a bath. I looked around to make sure we were alone, and then I propped the rifle against a boulder, took off my pistol, and laid it above the rifle. After I unleashed Bo, I waded into the water crutch, dog, clothes, and all. I knew it was foolish to wear my clothes into the water, but I just didn't care. The water was so inviting, and I thought it would help ease my mosquito bites for a little while, so I just waded in as soon as we got there. My clothes needed to be washed anyway. I started throwing a stick for

Bo, and we played for about an hour getting good and tired. It felt so good to get cooled off. I heard myself laughing, and I realized I hadn't laughed since the moose had tried to eat my clothes. It felt terrific! I dunked myself one more time before I hobbled out of the water. While Bo shook the water off himself, I shook the water off myself and wrung the water out of my clothes. After I fastened the leash on Bo, I picked up my rifle and slung the gun belt over my shoulder. Still laughing at Bo, I said, "Let's go home boy. Home! How sweet that sounds."

We made it back to camp without any trouble, but my ankle had begun to swell and hurt. I took off my wet clothes and hung them to dry. I brushed my hair and put on clean clothes. Then I took a towel and started rubbing Bo dry. As he snuggled close to me, I wondered once again what I would do without him.

After rubbing my ankle with the last little bit of liniment, I rewrapped it tightly and sat with my leg propped up to let my ankle rest. I wondered what I'd do for medicine after this. Even though my ankle was much better, it wasn't quite well. *So, I guess I will have to do like the Indians and use moss and mud,* I thought. *It might not help, but it won't hurt.*

After Bo and I had finished supper, I lay on the bed and tried to read one of the few books we were able to bring with us. I must have fallen asleep reading for when I woke up, it was dark out, and Bo was whining to be let out. Getting up I went to the door of the tent and let him out into the run. I was still afraid to let him outside the walls after dark. Bo ran around the wall investigating any suspicious spots. After letting Bo in I zipped up the tent door and made sure everything was secure for the night. Nighttime was the hardest time for me because there was so little I could do inside. Even if I was tired, I couldn't seem to rest without thinking of things I had to do the next day. I also missed Paul terribly in the evenings. We spent almost every evening sitting on the porch, or taking a walk talking over our day. Sometimes we would talk way into the night about our day or our plans for the next day about the boys, about our friends and family, and all of our dreams for the future. Oh, how I missed Paul.

Dear Diary

August 7
I haven't written anything in my diary, except the date, for four days because there has been very little to say. Today I found that I can put my full weight on my ankle, so tomorrow I'll start on the roof

again. But today I'll wash my clothes, get water, and cook a pot of soup. I may even make bread. I've had very little appetite lately, so maybe fresh bread and soup will help. I've gotten so tired of beans. I might even stew some dried apples and make a cobbler. I really need to use some of my sourdough starter and replenish it before it loses its strength. I've cooked so very little in the last month. I know that Bo and I will both enjoy a complete meal.

I've worked hard all this week. I've gotten the rest of logs on the roof. I nailed them at each end, and I managed to get the entire roof covered with wood. I'll soon be finished. I just need to get the tarp put on and the smaller logs in place so that it'll be waterproof.

Dear Diary

August 7
Now comes the hard part. I've got to get my large tarp onto the roof. I know I can't lift the tarp by myself when it's folded, so I'm going to try to pull it up using the ropes and pulleys. If that doesn't work, I'll unfold it and pull it up little by little. Then

I'll get it spread out as flat and even as I can. I've already got a few smaller trees cut to put in the valleys of the logs already covering the roof. I hope I can get all this done in one day, so if the wind gets up, the tarp won't blow off. I'll finish cutting all the smaller trees tomorrow and get them stripped and ready to go. Then, I'll tackle the tarp early the next morning. I still may put moss or sand up there, if I have the strength; it will make the cabin much warmer in the winter, and it might keep the snow and rain from pooling on the roof. I'm praying that I'm not here when winter comes, but I know I must prepare for it all the same.

Putting a tarp on a roof is definitely a two-person job. It took me all of one day just to get the tarp onto the roof and spread out flat. I planned to leave at least a six-inch flap overhanging each side of the cabin, and this made it even harder to lay the tarp out. After I had the tarp in place on the roof, I planned to nail the overhanging flaps onto the side walls of the cabin. I finally had to bring up a few of the smaller logs and use those to hold one end in place just to find out if the large tarp would be big enough. Thank goodness it was! At this point, I hoped it would only take one more day to finish. I was completely exhausted, but I still had to secure everything before I could stop for the night. I still had to bring a few more of the small logs up and I prayed that they would stay there all night. I hoped the wind wouldn't pick up because if it did, I might not have the heart to tackle this job again for weeks. I was ready to go to bed and sleep for weeks instead. I don't think I had ever been as exhausted as I was working on that roof.

Praise the Lord, when I went out the next morning, I saw that the wind hadn't taken my tarp! I just had to get everything squared up, and nailed down, so I decided to have an extra cup of coffee to give me the strength to finish the job. I couldn't take too long on my breakfast, though. The wind was calm in the mornings, but I needed to get as much done as possible before it kicked back up. Standing there nursing a cup of coffee wasn't getting anything done, so I finished it off and got started. First, I stood the remainder of the small logs against the wall. They were light enough that I was sure I would be able to pull them up from the low side of the roof.

After, I'd gotten everything I thought I'd need on the roof. I decided to start on the left side.

It was late in the evening when I finished, and I knew I should go down and feed Bo, but I just couldn't leave. I'd gotten the roof completely finished and I was just lying there marveling at the beauty of the sky. "Thank you, Lord, for the strength you've given me," I prayed. "Not just the physical strength, but the inner fortitude to keep going even when I thought it was impossible. The cabin is almost complete, and even if I don't do anything else to it, it'll be a secure home for Bo and me. If you give me the strength, I'm going to chink the walls, though. Otherwise, it will be too cold and drafty when hard winter comes. You know I don't want to be here for the winter, but I know you will provide no matter what."

Chapter 32

The next day, I began the hard and tiring job of chinking the walls with moss and mud. I'd spent a lot of my time, while I couldn't put weight on my ankle, hollowing out logs to hold water. I'd also split logs into planks and nailed them together to make boxes to fill with moss, dirt, and water to mix for the chinking. The boxes might have looked kind of funny because they weren't quite square, but I hoped they'd hold the mixture. I dug dirt from the forest because I didn't think sand from the beach would work. I used my sled to haul the dirt and the moss back to camp and dump them into separate piles. I had a good stockpile of the moss and soil on hand because I'd been digging and gathering them for weeks. I tried to bring back a sled full of either moss or dirt every time I went to the spring or foraging for fresh greens and berries. I prayed that my plan worked. I really wasn't sure if it would hold up to the weather, but I knew these were the best items I had to use for chinking.

I had to make four trips to the spring for water every morning. It took at least two trips to fill up each log. I filled my boxes with the dirt and moss and mixed in enough water to make the mixture stiff enough to hold together, but still pliable enough to press in between the logs. Each box would only mix enough chinking to do a small area. After a day of mixing one boxful at a time, I started mixing both boxes of chinking before I started applying it to the wall. That way, I didn't have to stop and mix another batch as quickly. At first, I had to go for more water at least three times each day because the water seeped out of the log, but by mixing both boxes at a time, I only had to go for water twice. It took a tremendous amount of the chinking mixture to complete one wall. It took me almost four days to finish just one wall, and I skimped a little toward the top, I got so impatient. I was just so ready to be done with that stinkin' chinkin'!

I had to redo the first areas I chinked because the mixture didn't hold together after it dried, but I finally got the recipe down pat. The chinking worked, but it was such hard work, and I knew my hands would never be the same. Even gloves didn't help much, and it didn't take long before they were unusable. So, I made some paddles almost like a spoon, which worked well, although I had to make new ones every few days because I would wear the end off of it pushing the chinking mixture between the logs. It was such slow going, I prayed that I would be through with this before the cold weather came. The nights were already getting cooler and, sometimes, I had to build a small fire in my camp stove even when I wasn't cooking, which meant that I was using up my firewood quicker than I expected. So, I decided that I'd chink one day, and the next day I'd cut and haul firewood. This wouldn't really give my arms and hands any rest, but it would change the monotony of the work. I also took a day to make myself a few pairs of gloves out of some of Paul's wool pants. They would help when I was chopping wood but wouldn't be any good for the chinking. The chinking had dried my hands out so badly that they hurt constantly. Even my lotion hadn't helped much, and I'd used almost all of it. I decided to try lard at night and wear gloves when I slept. I remembered my Grandmother doing this, and her hands were always soft. I didn't know if it would help, but I sure hoped it would.

Chapter 33

Dear Diary

August 8

It's been almost two weeks since I've visited Paul's grave. I don't feel quite as sad and lonely anymore, and I'm finally able to come here without the crushing grief weighing me down. It's almost a joy to be able to sit and talk to Paul. I tell him everything that I've been doing to the cabin. I know he would be proud of me for building the cabin and doing all that I have done so that Bo and I can survive. The cabin is almost finished! Sitting here, telling Paul about it, I can hardly believe it myself. Just a little more chinking, and it'll be ready for winter. Oh, please, Lord, please, let Todd and Joey find me before winter comes! I don't think I could bear it if I had to stay here all winter by myself!

As I sat there talking to Paul, I realized I had to start thinking about food for the winter, even though I prayed I wouldn't be here to need it. I knew that I had enough supplies to last for at least two or three more months, because I hadn't eaten as much as we would have had I been cooking for both Paul and me. But I had to be prepared for it, which meant I'd have to kill a deer.

I'd seen deer in the woods and closer to the boulders while I was cutting logs. But as time passed, and the threat of winter grew closer, I knew I had to prepare for anything that might happen. I would have to start scouting for deer trails in earnest. I knew I could kill a deer if I got a chance. I almost always hunted with Paul every winter, and even though it makes me a little sad every time I kill something, I always thank The Lord for giving me the skills to hunt and for providing the food. One time we hunted separately and we both got a deer, which gave us enough meat to share with my parents and some of our friends. We still had plenty for ourselves as well. The boys also hunted, and even though most years only one of us would be successful, we almost always had plenty of meat to last until the next fall. I knew this would be my best choice for meat for the winter.

Dear Diary

August 10
I could try to get a caribou if I can't get a deer. The caribou aren't much bigger than

a deer, so the meat won't go to waste if I get one. I haven't seen any close to the cabin, but we saw some along the river as we were getting to this area. This reminds me that I haven't really explored this area very well. I've really only gone as far as I've needed to, to find whatever it was I was searching for. I wonder if there's another clearing on the other side of the forest where I cut my trees, or somewhere above the boulders. Maybe Bo and I need to take a day or two and explore this area a little more. We'll do that if I can get past my fear of the bears, and if I don't get a deer before it really starts getting colder.

I've seen moose along the river as well as in the woods, but they are much bigger than I need for just Bo and me. I know I could try to kill a bear if I needed to, but like the moose, there would be much too much meat. And I'm not really certain if I could kill a bear. The way I reacted to the only ones I've ever seen makes me wonder if I could be calm enough to actually shoot one. Besides, I don't think I could ever get that much meat smoked, and I would hate for it to go to waste. I've tried fishing in the river, but it is too deep and fast moving where I am. I might be able to catch something if I took the boat out, but I don't think I can handle it by myself. Maybe if Bo and I do go exploring, we'll find a creek or a small inlet that has fish in it. Now that the cabin is nearly finished, I truly must take time to prepare for winter. I know subconsciously I've been putting it off because I can't even think that I may have to stay here past September, so the time has come to face the reality of my situation. But I can't let myself think that Bo and I will not be rescued before then, it hurts too much.

All at once I was stricken with the thought, *What if I'm not rescued! What if I'm doomed to live here for the rest of my life!* "Oh Lord!" I cried as I fell to my knees feeling like I had had the breath knocked out of me. I just knelt there moaning and rocking back and forth as I sobbed. "I just can't be here for the rest of my life, God! I just can't be! I can't bear the thought of not seeing my boys again! Oh, Lord, my supplies will never last over the winter, let alone for years! What will I do when they run out? I don't think there will ever be enough food for me to forage. What will I do then?" I asked.

Then I remembered the seed we had brought from home. We were going to plant them just to see if they would produce in the three months that we would be there. I had to find them! *I know we didn't leave them at home*, I thought as tried to calm myself and get up off the ground. Bo was going crazy. He was barking and running around and round me nudging me. Finally, he just sat down and howled. I tried to get a hold of him to assure him that I wasn't sick or going crazy, but he wouldn't let me touch him. When I was finally able to stand up, I stumbled and ran all the way to the cabin. The minute I got inside the cabin I started tearing everything apart. I couldn't find the seed anywhere. Finally, I slowed down my frantic search, and I took a careful look at the mess I had caused. I tried to find anything I hadn't looked through yet. I collapsed into a chair and concentrated on calming myself down.

As I scanned the room again, I saw Paul's duffel bag. It was under my bed, and it was the only thing in the entire tent that hadn't been moved or emptied. As I pulled it out and slowly opened it, I knew exactly where the seeds were. I removed everything until I came to his socks. There they were stuffed in a couple of pairs of Paul's socks. I just held them to my breast and cried. I remembered Paul telling me that he was going to put them there. He said his duffel had more room than mine, and he wanted to make sure the seeds were protected. His duffel was also waterproof, so that would help keep them safer than if they were in some of our other packages. Even though there weren't very many packs of seeds, there was a pack each of tomatoes, onions, cabbage, peas, squash, carrots and spinach. Finding the seed made me feel so much safer. "Lord," I prayed. "Why couldn't you have let me remember where these seeds were earlier? Was it really necessary to let me tear up my whole house looking for them?" I laughed as I prayed. "Oh, Lord, thank you again for allowing me to find these seeds. Now I know that if for some reason rescue doesn't come, I will be able to have a small garden next spring. Thank you for always providing even when I don't realize it."

The next day instead of working on the cabin, I went down to the little creek to look for watercress and to see if there were any fish there. I told myself that if I found fish there, I would bring the fishing gear the next time I came to forage. I couldn't believe I'd been so blind as to never even look for fish there. I'd been gathering watercress along with mushrooms there all summer. There were also a good many edible mushrooms in this area, I decided to dry some of them for winter. I also picked other greens like fiddlehead ferns, dandelions, and nettles to help supplement my diet. They make an excellent salad and are good in soups too. I was happy to find some of the same things that grew around the creeks and rivers back home. Every time we would go to the woods or to the river, the boys and I would see who could gather the most greens and mushrooms to add to our lunch. I didn't find any fish in that creek. So, I decided that I'd go to the inlet where I bathe the next day and look for fish there.

I'd seen berry patches, but so far I hadn't gathered very many because they weren't quite ripe enough and because I was afraid of the bears. I'd only seen those two since I'd been there, but both times, it scared me to death. I knew I had to gather some of the berries before they were all gone, bears or no bears. I had to come to terms with the fact that we were sharing this place. I couldn't continue to let them scare me into submission. I had to get stronger and braver where they were concerned. My supplies were holding out fine, but I didn't want to waste the opportunity to eat fresh fruits and vegetables while they were available. A few fresh blueberries would be great to eat, and they were an excellent source of vitamins. I've also seen what looks like raspberries and wild strawberries. There's no reason the bears should get them all. I still had plenty of flour and sugar, but I knew they wouldn't last, so I decided that I would make a cobbler when I finally got brave enough to go berry picking. I had probably already missed out on the strawberries, because I'd been such a coward. I knew Bo would let me know if there was a bear, or any other animal around. I had to learn to rely on him more.

Chapter 34

I finished chinking the cabin, and I was pleased with the work I had done, but I hadn't realized that it would make the inside of the cabin and tent so very dark. Now, I had to figure out what to do about that. I thought about taking down the tent, but I knew it would be much warmer to leave it up just in case I was here when winter came. I also thought about cutting a couple of windows, but I didn't have anything to cover them with. Maybe, if I killed a deer, I could somehow cure the hide and scrape it thin enough to use for windowpanes. I could cut out windows and put up shutters, but I'd have to think about that. If I did cut out windows and put up shutters, it would be fine to have them open while I was here, but if I went to get water or anything else, and forgot to close them the squirrels and voles would have free reign of my cabin. I don't know what I'd do if I came home to find all of my supplies scattered and ruined. Bo has spent many a night chasing the voles out or killing them if he's fast enough. He's also really good at keeping the squirrels chased off. I finally decided to leave the window issue for another day. I needed to split a long log and shape it, so it'll slide into the brackets on either side of my door.

My door will be much more secure with the bar in place.

Dear Diary

August 12
For over a week I've felt that there is something wrong. I keep looking behind me thinking that there is something there, but nothing ever is. I'm so nervous I jump at any little noise. Maybe I'm just paranoid, but every day I take my binoculars and gun and go to the river. I sometimes go three or more times a day hiding and watching for what I don't know. I don't think it's just me; Bo's been very edgy also although that might be because of me. I sometimes wonder what he thinks. I know he must think I'm crazy sometimes because I talk to him and ask him questions and his opinion as if I expect him to answer. Sometimes I think maybe I'm going mad because I talk to myself. But I think it's just the need to hear someone's voice. Perhaps this feeling is caused by the change in the weather. It's gotten colder in the evenings, even though it's only August. I keep watching the sky thinking maybe it's going to storm

although I see very few clouds. I've tried to rest more and eat more often thinking that might be part of my problem. Or, maybe it's just because I've finished the cabin, and I don't have enough work to keep me busy. I don't know what's causing this feeling, but I sure hope it passes soon. I don't know how much more I can stand.

I know my fears must not keep me from gathering berries if there are still any to be had, anxious feeling or no anxious feeling. It's gotten so bad that I make sure I have the rifle with me even in the yard. And my pistol is always on my hip. I just automatically put it around my waist each morning as I dress. I've started watching for tracks everywhere we go. I'm beginning to think maybe it is wolves Bo smells although we haven't seen any tracks, and he's not acting like there's another threatening animal close by. Whatever this feeling is, it needs to hurry up and pass on by. I'm exhausted by the middle of the day just from constantly being on edge. Eerie feeling or not, today I'm taking my buckets and Bo and we're going to the berry patch. It's about a mile behind the cabin, and hopefully, this black mood will lift on our walk.

It was a clear day, and the view along the path was wonderful. The wild blueberries were beautiful. We timed our berry-picking day just right. Most of the berries were ripe. They were so fat and juicy. It didn't look like the bears knew this patch was there. I didn't see any sign that any animals, except the magpies, had been feeding off this patch. I picked and filled each of the buckets with berries, and probably could have filled another with the amount I ate. I saw no sign of a bear or any creature other than birds. I finally felt the anxiety slipping away. Bo was stretched out sleeping in the sun, the sky was crystal clear, I picked enough berries to last for weeks, and I ate enough to satisfy my sweet tooth for several days.

When I got back to camp, I spread the berries out to dry on a couple of planks placed over some sawhorses. They made a fine makeshift table. I had laid a couple of Paul's old shirts over the planks before I spread the berries out to dry. Then I draped mosquito netting over the berries hoping to keep the bugs and birds from eating them. This should work, I thought. Even though I cut quite a few trees around my cabin, there was still very little direct sunlight in the yard. Because of this, I knew it would take two or three days for them to dry. I'd need to check them every day and pick out the bad ones. I also had to take them in each evening. That way I hoped to be able to keep them out of the animals' reach. I wanted to get them packaged up when they were dry. I planned to go again the next day to pick more berries. I wanted to gather and dry as many as I could while they were available. They would be a wonderful treat in the months to come. I thought I'd also use some of the fresh berries to make a pie, although I hated to use so much of my precious sugar and flour to make a dessert just for me. I'd been trying to make them last as long as possible just in case I was here longer than I thought I would be.

I guess I knew my luck wouldn't hold. The next day, as I came close to the berry patch, I used my binoculars to see if it was all clear. There in the middle of the patch were not one, but three bears. There, in my blueberry patch, was a mother bear and her two half-grown cubs making themselves at home, eating all my berries. I just stood there watching and holding on to Bo. Even with his leash he nearly pulled me over several times. He was so upset with me. He could see and smell the bears, and he wanted to run them out of our berry patch. I kept telling him, they would just eat him instead of the berries. I told him to be quiet. I thanked The Lord again for sending me a dog that didn't bark much, but Bo was making almost as much noise as a bark with his growling and whining, I just knew the bears were going to hear him any minute.

Even though I was terrified, I stood there watching for a little while thinking of how beautiful the bears were. I wished that I had brought my camera along with the buckets. I stood watching for a few more minutes before going back to camp. I knew of two more berry patches in the area I'd explored, and I should be able to find them with the help of the maps I drew when I first went in search of a good campsite. I decided to try them the next day even though they were farther into the woods and closer to the boulders.

Chapter 35

As we got back to camp, I knew something was wrong. Bo was frantic and almost pulled my arm from its socket. I quickly knelt and pulled him close to me. I told him he must be quiet. As I sat my buckets down, I raised my rifle and checked to make sure it was loaded. I also unsnapped the holster that held my pistol. I made a wide circle around the cabin so that I would be able to see who or what was there, but I didn't see anything out of the ordinary. As I eased in closer, I saw the scratches on the door, and when I looked down, I saw bear tracks, very large bear tracks! It had to be a brown bear because I'd seen black bear tracks, and these were twice as big as those!

I knew then I'd made a mistake, by putting the berries inside the cabin walls. The bear could smell the berries and was trying to get them. I suppose he wasn't too hungry, or I might not have a door left. And I also knew there was a good chance he'd be back, and that I must be very watchful. After checking the door to make sure the hinges were still secure, I took my berries, inside the tent and put them inside one of my tin containers. I hoped that maybe if he couldn't smell them, he wouldn't bother to come back again. I hated to think about missing out on the rest of the berries, but I had to get these dry before I could chance going to gather more. I still had to put the berries out on the planks every day until they were dry, but I'd stay here and pray that the bear didn't come back. If it did, I'd have to kill it. I knew enough about them to know that if he had decided this was where he could get food, he'd keep coming back. Hopefully, he was discouraged enough that he wouldn't come back. I honestly didn't want to shoot him. It was still too warm, and there would be too much meat for just Bo and myself.

Dear Diary

August 15
I don't know what to do with Bo, he's so angry with me, he has walked back and forth, and around, the tent at least a hundred times. He won't even look at or listen to me. I made him stay inside while I secured everything outside and made sure that we have enough water inside the cabin for a couple of days. Now, even though Bo has settled down, he still won't even look at me. I lay awake most of the night, with my gun by my side, listening for any sound of the bear. I didn't hear anything except the rustling of the leaves,

and the voles scurrying around. Maybe he didn't feel the berries were worth his effort. I pray this is so. When morning came, I took my guns and went outside leaving a furious and upset Bo inside. I walked all around the cabin and the yard, but I didn't see any sign of the bear other than the set of tracks that he left yesterday. The tracks lead into the woods, and I know if Paul were here, he'd track the bear to its den. If it were near the cabin, he'd probably kill it. But Paul isn't here, and I'm not that brave. I'll just have to be more careful not to leave anything out where he might smell it and pray that he doesn't come back. Thank you, God, for keeping us safe!

It was about nine o'clock, almost time for bed, and we hadn't seen any sign of the bear all day. I spread the berries out to dry again and did some chores that I'd been putting off. I even let Bo outside for a little while. He thoroughly examined the bear tracks and marked everywhere the bear had been, but he didn't try to leave the yard. I had just finished putting away my dishes for the evening and settled down to read for a while when Bo went on alert. I knew the bear was back! I quickly tied Bo to the table leg although I knew that it wouldn't hold him if he really wanted to get free! I grabbed the rifle and sat down beside him talking to him quietly trying to calm him down.

We could hear the bear growling and grumbling outside! I had my pistol on the table but kept the rifle in my hand. He was clawing on the door and pushing on it! I prayed, "Please, Lord, let the crossbar hold!" I really didn't want to shoot the bear, but I would if I had to. Paul had always told me to make sure to shoot a bear between the eyes, or in the heart because if you don't, you might not kill it. I was terrified! I didn't know whether I could hold the gun steady enough to shoot him! "Please, God, give me the strength to shoot straight!" I prayed.

I think the bear has given up, I thought, feeling relief. I hadn't heard a sound for a while, and Bo had settled down, but he was still angry. I finally moved from the floor, and I stretched out on the bed with Bo on one side and my gun on the other. I didn't want to go to sleep, but I was completely drained, both emotionally and physically. Bo had finally gone to sleep and was snoring loudly, but I still just lay there listening, unable to rest.

The bear came back three nights in a row. After the first night, I took the door off the hinges and turned it around because the bear had almost pushed it in that first night. By turning it around, the door would open out instead of swinging in. When I turned the door around, I had to completely change the door frame. My crossbar was built onto the door, so I had to move it back inside, and move the bracket it rests in, to the other side of the frame. I hoped that by turning the door around, it wouldn't be as easy for the bear to push it down. I also nailed the door shut each night. I knew it might not make any difference if the bear really wanted to get inside, but it made me feel more secure.

Dear Diary

August 17
I know now that he is not after the few berries. He's after Bo and me. I don't dare go very far from camp, but today I had to go get water. I left Bo in the tent knowing that I wouldn't be able to hold him and shoot the bear if it should show up. We've made a well-beaten path to the spring, and it's only about a quarter of a mile from the cabin.

I ran as fast as I could to the spring and filled my buckets. Then walked as quickly as I could back to the cabin. My heart was beating so fast and loud it sounded like a drum in my ears! I was so scared, I felt as if I would explode at any minute! I knew I needed to slow down because I was sloshing water out with every step. At that rate, I thought I'd just have to turn around and go back for more water, but I just couldn't slow down! I was hoping and praying that I could somehow manage to keep at least half the water in the buckets!

I don't know why I didn't take the sled and my five-gallon tin can. After the incident with the wolverine, I had taken my dried beans out of the tin can and stored the beans in some of my waterproof bags. I had started using the can for water just so I wouldn't have to make so many trips to the spring. Now, I wished I had thought to bring it. It had a lid that didn't leak once it was secured onto the can. I wouldn't have to worry about losing so much water if I had thought to bring it. I was so afraid of the bear that I wasn't thinking straight! Now, because of my fear, I'd have to go back the next day for more water! Lord, help me!

I was so scared for Bo! If the bear killed me, Bo would be locked in the cabin unable to get out! "Please, Please, God," I prayed, "don't let the bear show up! Please let me get back to the cabin!" I knew if anything happened to Bo it would be my fault! I shouldn't have been so selfish! I shouldn't have brought him to Alaska with me! My heart just aches when I think that, although he has been my salvation, because I surely would have gone crazy without him, and now I might be the cause of his death! Oh, what a horrible thought! "Please, Lord, protect Bo!"

Dear Diary

August 17
I think the bear has finally given up. He hasn't been here in four nights, but I am still so scared. I continually look around and listen for the bear, and I'm not about to let my guard down. I still lead Bo wherever we go, and I make sure we're back in camp well before dark. I even make sure Bo and I are well away from camp before we use the bathroom, and I make sure it's covered well. I hope that the bear will not smell it. I hope that I've done enough. I've tried to think of everything I can do. Today I even made a broom of cedar boughs and swept all around our camp trying to erase the bear's tracks and ours. I know I can't do this every day, but I'll surely try even though it might not help. I want to be better prepared if he or another bear comes back, so using my

brace and bit, I drilled holes making a long slot in the door. It's just high enough for me to see outside and I made sure it's large enough for my gun barrel to fit through. I also drilled slots on either side of the door, and in every other wall of the cabin. I'm so thankful that I hadn't cut the windows out yet because if I had the bear might've been able to pull or push an entire wall down. I pray that the bear has truly moved on, but if not, I hope the slots help me get a good shot at the bear's heart, or through his head, if I must kill it.

Chapter 36

We had several days with no indication that the bear was anywhere around. I'd begun to relax a little. I'd taken my sled and made two trips to the spring for water. I filled everything I could with water. I'd also let Bo go without his leash the last couple of days thinking the bear had lost interest. We'd just finished supper when we heard the grumbling and growling. The bear was back! My heart just filled with fear and dread knowing that the time had come. I must kill the bear! I turned to Bo and hugged him close. "Well boy I am going to have to kill this bear," I said. Bo ran to the door growling loudly. Every hair on his back was standing straight up. He wanted out! He looked back at me as if to say, open this door and let me out, I'll take care that old bear! Good ole Bo, he would defend me to the death I thought as I reached down and hugged him again.

Before we had left home on this trip, Paul and I had practiced with both rifles, his and mine, and with the pistols. He made sure I could handle whichever gun was available. He wanted us to be able to load and use the guns without having to take a lot of time thinking about it. I'm a much better shot with the pistol than either of the rifles, but the pistol wouldn't do this job. Paul assured me that my Remington .350 Magnum would kill any bear if you shoot it through the heart or right between the eyes. "Please, Lord, please, give me the strength to do this!" I prayed. "Please let my aim be straight and true." As I picked up my rifle, I tried to plan what I might do if I didn't kill it with one shot. I knew there was nothing more dangerous than shooting a bear and not killing it. The thought that I might not kill it made me so scared I felt nauseous. "Please, dear Lord, please help me!"

I tied Bo to the table leg inside the tent, and I begged him to please, please, please stay there! I hoped and prayed that it would be sturdy enough to hold him. Then I eased out of the tent and over to the door of the cabin. I peeped through the slot watching the bear! *Oh, my dear Lord, it's a grizzly!* I gasped, as I watched him. He was standing straight up just walking around, grumbling, and turning over everything that was in his way! It hurt me to think that I'd have to kill that magnificent creature, but I knew he'd never go away, and I was sick and tired of living in fear of it! *So, I will kill him,* I thought. *If he comes to the door, and I can get a good shot. I'll just do it.* I could scarcely catch my breath. I was so afraid! I felt as if my whole body was trembling! I put my head against the wall and prayed. I tried to steady my nerves. I knew that I had to kill this beast, or he would kill us.

The bear was banging on the door! I was standing so close to it that I could smell it! It stunk so bad it made me gag! I could feel the door giving with each push! I looked out, and I could see he was much taller than the door! Propping the rifle barrel in the slot, I tried to gauge where his heart might be. I stood there for a few minutes closing my eyes begging God to help me. Then taking a deep breath and letting it out slowly, I pulled the trigger.

All at once, Bo was there! He was jumping at the door, and he was mad, mad, mad! He got between me and the door, so I couldn't get close enough to look out the slot. I quickly got my rifle ready to shoot again, if I had to! I tried to calm Bo, but he wouldn't listen to me! I pushed him away from the door, so he began trying to dig under the wall. I had never seen him so angry! I finally managed to get to the door and look outside. There, lying on the ground was the bear! It looked as if he had just backed up and fallen over! I stood there frozen, peeping out through the slot in the door just watching as the bear thrashed his legs about! I didn't dare go out yet! I needed to know that he was really dead, so I waited.

I could see that Bo was barking, but I realized I couldn't hear him! "Oh, dear Lord," I begged, "Please let my hearing return! Please don't let me be deaf! Oh please, don't let it be permanent!" After what seemed like an eternity, my hearing slowly started to return. Bo still sounded like he was barking from the depths of a well, but at least I could hear him. I laughed knowing that my hearing loss wasn't permanent, and it was because I'd shot the gun inside the cabin. I'd had no choice. I had to kill that bear! This was just another lesson I'd had to learn the hard way. If I ever had to discharge a gun inside a building again, I would make sure my ears were covered.

All at once, my legs gave way, and I was sitting on the ground! I reached for Bo and hugged him to me. He kept trying to get away from me so he could keep trying to dig under the wall. He wanted outside! He wanted that bear! I kept talking to him trying to calm him down, but he wasn't having any of that. I told him that we would go outside soon and see the bear, but we must make sure it was dead first. I don't think that Bo believed me. I scolded him and made him stop digging, but he was still angry with me. Poor little Bo. He believed I was just being mean and keeping him from his job.

It had been over an hour since the bear had moved before I decided it was safe to go out and make sure he was truly dead. As I pulled the nails out of the door, I kept looking through the slit to make sure he still wasn't moving. I dragged Bo back into the tent so I could tie him back to the table leg. When I got there, I realized he had slipped out of his collar, and that was how he'd gotten loose. I slipped his collar back on, and tightened it, then tied him back to the leg. I hoped that would hold him until I knew it would be safe for him to come outside.

I made sure the gun was ready to fire before I stepped outside. As I got closer, I could see that the bear wasn't breathing. I fell to my knees and thanked God for His protection and for giving me the ability to kill the bear. At first, I thought I would wait until morning before skinning it. I knew that I must cut his throat and let him bleed, like Paul taught me when we killed a deer, even if I didn't clean it that night. I knew that it wouldn't be good to leave it overnight, but I just didn't know if I could tackle the job in the middle of the night. It needed to be done as soon as possible after the animal was killed, so I took a deep breath and Paul's skinning knife and moved closer to the bear. As I stood looking down at him, it seemed as if he was looking at me. I just stood there paralyzed with fear. Even though I could see that it wasn't breathing, and his eyes weren't moving, it still seemed as if he was looking at me. After a long moment and another prayer of thanks, I turned to get to work. As I took a step back, I tripped and fell on the bear. I landed hard on his outstretched arm, and its paw scratched my arm! At that moment, I completely forgot that he was dead! I screamed! I just knew that the bear had grabbed me! He wasn't dead after all! He had just been playing possum! "Oh, Lord! Please don't let me die like this!" I could hear Bo furiously trying to get out of the cabin! "Lord Please, Oh Please, don't let me die! Please! I must take care of Bo! I can't leave him here alone!"

I finally gained control of my arms and legs and rolled off the bear. I quickly jumped to my feet, but I lost my balance, and I stumbled back. I sat flat down with a plop far out of reach of the bear. I sat there dazed for a few minutes, and then I started giggling like a little girl. Falling on the bear had scared me almost to death, but now all I could do was sit there laughing hysterically. I was laughing so hard tears were running down my face! Inside the cabin, Bo was still going crazy. Slowly, I got up and went to the door. I was still laughing so hard my sides hurt, and I could barely get the door open. When I finally did, I let him out to see the bear. It was the only fair thing to do. He immediately attacked it! He was growling and fighting it with everything his little body had. I know he thought he was killing it for me, and I let him fight until he was completely worn out. Even after he was so tired, he could hardly move he wouldn't leave. He simply crawled up on top of the bear and pranced around like he was the king of the mountain. When I look back on this time, I wish I had gone and gotten my camera. What a picture that would have been. My brave little Bo protecting me from this monster! After Bo decided the monsters had all been taken care of, he wandered back to the cabin door and stationed himself there like any good guard dog would. I turned back to the job at hand and went to the bear to slit its throat.

Chapter 37

I changed my mind. I decided it might not be such a good idea to wait until morning. I was too keyed up to sleep, and I was already dirty from my wrestling match with the bear, so I decided to go ahead and get the job started. I needed to get him skinned and everything taken care of before any other predators came prowling around. So, even though it was almost midnight, I gathered my tools and got to it.

I built a large bonfire on either side of the yard. I hoped they would keep other predators away. I had my rifle leaning against a tree within easy reach and the revolver on my hip as I started skinning the bear. I knew I had to cut his head off first. I was glad to get rid of it, too, because his eyes still seemed to be watching me. I tried to close them several times, but they would slowly reopen every time, which just freaked me out. I even tried throwing an old shirt over it, but for some reason, it just kept sliding off. So, the head must go as quickly as I could possibly make it go!

Cutting the bear's head off was one of the hardest things I think I had done in all my life. I had to use a knife, the ax, and the saw. I don't know how many times I had to stop, lean my head against a tree to throw up, and pray for strength. I was convinced that I would never get the smell of blood and bear out of my head! Finally, I got the head off! I just couldn't stand those eyes looking at me another minute, so I picked the head up and put it in one of the boxes that I had built. I had to almost hug the thing to me it was so heavy. I'll bet it weighed fifty pounds! Because it bothered me so much, I dragged the box well away from the cabin, and completely out of sight before I started skinning the carcass.

It took me the rest of the night and well into the morning to finish skinning and cleaning the bear. I wished I'd paid more attention to how my father did it when I was younger. He'd killed and cleaned hogs on the farm every year. Even though I'd helped Paul skin and clean deer every year when we'd killed one, he did most of the work. The only thing I've ever shot and had to clean by myself was a rabbit. And that was a long time ago.

I was ten years old when I got my first gun for Christmas. I'd begged for one for months, and I was so excited when I unwrapped it. My Dad said that he believed that girls should learn to shoot a gun the same as boys. But also just like the boys, if they went hunting and killed something, they should know how to skin and clean whatever they killed. The first time I went hunting with Dad and my brother, I shot a rabbit. I was so proud of myself that was until I remembered Dad's rule: if you kill it, you clean it. Not only did I cry when I shot that poor little rabbit but having to clean it by myself was horrible. Needless to say, this broke me from begging to go hunting until I was much older. Every member of my family knew how to shoot and use every gun on the farm. My Dad and Grandpa made sure of this. He said that everyone needed to be able to confidently use whatever gun was at hand if and when it was needed.

We always had some sort of predator sneaking around the farm, and he couldn't guarantee that a man would always be there to take care of it. So, we had target practice at least once a month. It became a fun family gathering time over the years. We'd pack a picnic lunch and go to the creek or somewhere else on the property. We'd eat, then set up the targets, and the competition would begin. Thinking back on that now, I'm so glad I had the upbringing I did. Without the self-reliance that my parents instilled in me, I would've never been able to survive here this long by myself.

How I wished I didn't have to clean the bear so close to the cabin. But it was much too heavy for me to move. One of the reasons it took me so long just to skin the bear was because I had to stop and sharpen the knife ever little bit. Most likely it was because I really didn't know how to sharpen it right to begin with. That's just one more thing I wished I hadn't left for Paul to do.

After I got the bear skinned, I had to gut it. So, I split it open, and as I was reaching inside to pull all the organs out, I wondered what the boys would think of their mother with her arms elbow deep inside the cavity of a bear. Just the thought of Joey's face made me laugh. Once again, I was laughing so hard I was crying. Then, all at once, I was trembling and shaking violently all over! My legs felt as if they wouldn't hold me up, and it was all I could do to get to the fire and sit down on a stump! My laughter was replaced by a terrible heaving in my stomach, and I was suddenly violently ill. After the sickness passed, I slowly slid to the ground. I could feel myself sinking, and I thought I must surely be dying. "Lord, please don't let me die like this," I begged weakly. "What about Bo?" I asked. "He can't survive without me!" My prayers faded as the world turned black and I lost consciousness.

I don't know how long I was out. But, as I regained consciousness, I thought I heard my daddy calling me. He was saying, "Julie, get up! You must finish what you've started! You killed that bear, now get up and finish cleaning it!" I could hear myself saying, "Okay, Daddy," as I tried to get up. But I couldn't move. It was as if my arms and legs were too heavy to move. I lay there for what seemed like hours trying to pull myself together. Over and over, I kept telling myself I had to finish cleaning the bear. When I could finally sit up, I looked around expecting to see my daddy standing there watching me. When I had regained my composure, I thanked God, knowing he had sent Daddy back to save me. To this day, I'm sure that I would have died there if Daddy hadn't called me back.

As I got up, I said to myself, "I need coffee." So, I stumbled into the cabin and poured myself a cup of leftover, cold coffee. I just turned the cup up and drank it in almost one swallow. I stood there breathing deeply while I automatically refilled the pot with water and coffee to make another pot. I knew I would need it before the day was over. When I set my cup down, I realized my hands and arms were covered in the blood and gore from the bear. I just stood there looking at my bloody limbs as if they were not part of my body. I continued looking at them then thought, *Oh well, I wasn't through with cleaning the bear anyway*, so I picked up the tripod, took it out to the fire, set it

up over the hot coals, and hung the coffee pot to
boil.

Chapter 38

Bo was so delighted! He had done everything from attacking the bear to rolling in the blood before he had grown tired of all the activity. When he'd finished, he just lay there and watched me. After he'd had his fun, and I'd had another cup of coffee and some breakfast, I decided it was time to start the next part of the job. I picked up the saw and slowly went back to the bear. I had to give myself a pep talk just to have the strength to pick up that saw. I knew the job had to be finished, and nobody else was going to do it, and once again, I could hear my daddy's words echoing in my ears, "This is your job, Julie, so get on with it. It's not going to go away."

It took hours, but I finally finished cleaning the bear. I butchered it the best I could, and with the ropes and pulleys, I hung the hams and shoulders as high as possible in the trees. I trimmed as much fat off as possible and stored it in every available container I had. I planned on rendering it out for lard over the next few days. I cut as much meat as I could off the ribs and back. Then I cut this into strips so that I could dry it on a smoker. I wrapped it in one of the small tarps and hung it up beside the hams and shoulders. It was early morning, and I'd been at this for over twenty-four hours. I was more exhausted than I think I'd ever been, but I wouldn't allow myself more than a few minutes rest time. I knew if I stopped for very long, it would probably be another full day and night before I woke up. I couldn't stop for that long because I had to finish cleaning up the area where I cleaned the bear.

As I stood there looking at the carnage around me, it was hard to decide what to do first. Since the head and intestines were already boxed up, I decided to take care of those first. So, I took the sled over to where I left the boxes and got them loaded up. As I was doing this, I thought I might just add the hide and throw it all away, but then I decided that I might need the hide. So, I'd deal with it later. I dragged the sled down to the river and dumped the boxes. I hoped everything would wash far downstream, but if they didn't, the eagles and ravens would soon have them taken care of. Then I made sure the boxes were completely clean. I didn't want anything to come sniffing around them or the cabin. Next, I moved the fire and ashes over to where I had killed the bear. Then l put more wood on it and let it burn; I hoped it would take the blood and bear smell away from the area. Then I swept up any other debris from the butchering and threw it into the fire.

I knew that I couldn't stop for long, but I realized that I was famished, and Bo had to be hungry, too. So, I quickly made myself some peanut butter and crackers and fed Bo. Just that small break had me nodding off, so I drank the last cup of coffee. It was very strong because it had been simmering for hours over the remains of the fire. Before I made myself go back to work, I made a fresh pot and made sure Bo had water in his bowl.

My arms were so tired they were shaking. It took everything I had left to get the hide hung and stretched. I had to drag it well away from the cabin, and I bet it weighed a hundred pounds. Thank God I had the sled! After what felt like another day and a half, I finally succeeded in getting the hide hung and stretched in the trees. I got it as high and as tight as I could, and I'd work on cleaning it over the next few days. Or, maybe I'd just cut it down, dig a hole and bury it. That's really what I'd like to do, but I wouldn't because I knew I might need the hide before I was rescued.

Dear Diary

August 19

I think I've finally come to a point where it'll be safe for me to stop. So, Bo and I are going to eat and get some much-needed sleep.

Dear Diary

August 19
I slept the rest of that night and most of the next day. I knew I needed to get to the task of drying the meat, but since it was so late, I decided that the chore could wait until morning. I'm going to cook a good meal for Bo and myself. But first, I'm going to go take a bath! I can't stand the smell of blood and bear for one more minute!

Chapter 39

I worked three days building a rack and hanging the stripped meat to air dry. I rubbed what little salt, I thought I could spare, on the meat hoping it would help to cure it and make it more edible. There was so much meat, I tried to think of everything I could to preserve it. I've also rendered out most of the fat over the last few days. It's such slow work with only my big iron pot and a frying pan. I've put the grease in everything I can find to hold it. I had so few empty containers that I had to empty my rice into a waterproof bag so I could use the can it was in. Thank goodness I had washed and saved all the used food cans. I never could have imagined that any animal could have that much fat on it. I knew if I didn't render the fat meat it wouldn't keep long, and as it is, I'd have to throw over half of the fat away. I hated the thought of wasting any of it, but I had more than I could've used in several years already stored.

Bo really enjoyed the fresh meat, but I was having a hard time eating it. Maybe I'd enjoy it better if I ever got the disgusting smell of the bear's blood out of my head. I knew if I cared for the meat the right way it would last us all winter, and into next year. I Thanked God every night for the meat, but I also prayed that I wouldn't need it after September. Even though I'd done all I could to be prepared to stay here through the winter, I honestly couldn't let myself think about being here past the middle of September. I just didn't think I could handle it if the month came and went without the boys finding me.

Instead of throwing all the extra fat away, I decided to make lye soap with some of it. I remembered as a child helping my Mother and Grandmother make it. I hoped I could remember all the steps. I had to make the lye water first by pouring water over some of the ashes from my fire. The water had to seep through the ashes to become lye water. I would have to put small holes in the bottom of one of my buckets to make the lye water, and that would be a sacrifice, but it couldn't be helped. After that, I'd melt some of the fat and mix the lye water with it using one of the wooden spoons I made when I was chinking the walls. I had to be cautious not to let any of the lye water get on me because it's acidic and I knew it would burn me badly. When I get it mixed properly, I planned to pour it in some of the smaller boxes I made while I was recuperating from the sprained ankle. Then, once it hardened, if it did, I could cut it into bars. Even if it didn't harden, I'd still have a soft soap that I could use to wash dishes and clothes with. It's incredible the things I remembered from when I was a child.

I also smoked the hams and shoulders. I made a teepee smoker by wrapping a tarp around some poles that I stuck in the ground and tied together at the top. Then I took smaller branches and lashed together a platform to hang the meat from. After I had finished that, I dug a hole for a fire pit just outside the tent. I had to keep the fire going night and day to make enough coals. Then I put the coals in a trench that I dug into the center of the teepee to smoke. I had to cover the trench with slabs of wood to hold in the smoke so it would rise over the meats. I hoped this would work. I couldn't remember exactly how long it would take for them to be completely smoked, but oh well! I had nothing else to do and plenty of time.

It'd been ten days since I'd killed the bear. I took some of Paul's clothes and cut them up to make bags to store the dried meat in. We should have enough meat to last Bo and me at least a year if it kept. I hung them in the tent, and it amazed me how much meat there was. The hams had turned out nicely and were ready to wrap in the bags and hang in the walkway around the tent where they'd stay cool and dry.

I took a long log and drilled twelve holes in it. Each hole was about eight inches deep. I'd decided to try making candles with some of the lard. For wicks, I took strips of fabric and twisted them together then dipped them in wax from a couple of candle stubs that I melted. I dipped the wicks a few times letting them dry in between each dipping; they should work like a regular candle wick. I could melt some of the bear lard and gently pour it around the wicks in each mold and let it sit until it hardened. I hoped this would work so I would have extra candles. If it didn't work, I would try melting one of my remaining candles in with the fat. That way maybe it would harden. If the candles didn't work, I knew I could make oil lamps using the lard and a wick. I would have to give up one of my bowls or cups to make the oil lamp, but when winter came, I knew I'd rather have the light than an extra cup.

Dear Diary

August 26
I really hope the candles or oil lamps work because I don't have very many wax candles left. I want to make as many candles as possible because of the months of almost total darkness. If I have to make oil lamps, I won't be able to make very

many. I just don't have enough containers for them. I know I'll go mad without enough light, and I can make plenty of candles, so I really hope they work. It's the madness that scares me the most. Just thinking about it scares me to death. I just don't think I can survive the darkness. I'm afraid I'll be confined to the cabin with very little to do to occupy my time, and I can't stand the thought of it being gloomy and dark on top of that. "Please Lord, let the boys come for me before then! Please don't leave me here through the winter!"

Chapter 40

I tried to think of everything I could make with the bear lard. The candles were a success, and I made dozens of them. I also stored away some lard to make more, but there was still plenty for other projects. So, I decided to try making windowpanes with some of the lard and a few sheets of paper from my sketchbook. I hadn't cut out my windows yet, but I'd planned on doing it before I had to deal with the bear. I'd been putting it off because I didn't want to make any more openings for the mosquitoes and squirrels to come through. But if I had windowpanes, where they wouldn't get in, I could go ahead and cut them out.

After quite a few failures, I finally had eight windowpanes that I thought would work. I rubbed the sketchbook paper with enough grease to saturate it, and then I let it dry for a couple of days. After that, I lightly scraped it and greased it again. I hoped by doing that it would work the grease deep into the fibers of the paper and make it stronger. I repeated these steps two or three times, and finally, I had something that I thought would work for a windowpane. I decided to make frames to hold the panes, and then I would start making shutters for the windows. I'd wait until I had everything ready to put in place before I cut the openings in the walls of the cabin. The shutters would be made from some smaller limbs nailed to a sturdy frame. I used strips of leather from Paul's boots for hinges, and I made brackets for a drop bar to go on either side of each window. This way, I could close them securely at night or in stormy weather. I decided to place one window in each of the walls of the cabin. Even though I couldn't see through the panes, light would come through them. It would be good to have some natural light coming in because even when I had the door open, it was terribly gloomy inside the cabin most days. I prayed the windows would help.

With the extra panes, I planned to make a covering for the rifle slot in the door. I had to figure out a way to make it secure in a storm, but easily removable if I should have to use that slot again. I'd decided to cut the windows out where the slots were in the walls. They were at good height, and it made it easier to get the saw started. I knew that if anything should attack the cabin again, I would have to break out some of the panes, but I would deal with that when it happened. I also knew the panes might not last long, but now that I knew how to make them, I would be able to replace them as needed.

Chapter 41

Dear Diary

September 1
It's the first day of September, and I know if the boys don't hear from us at eight o'clock tonight, they will soon be looking for us. I can just picture the boys and Amy gathered at the house tonight, and I can see the anxious worry on their faces when we don't call. Joey will be practical about it all. He's always been the more rational one. Todd will be ready to jump in the car right then and come find us. Oh, how I hope Amy can help keep him calm enough to listen to reason. I am hopeful Joey and Amy will be able to overrule Todd's impulses and start working on what to do next. If they are, Joey will be able to start the process of filing the necessary reports. He'll know that they'll need to wait at least a day or two just in case we are running behind. He won't be really concerned for at least three days, but all that time, he'll be making plans and getting things ready to start a search. I know they'll all begin worrying tonight, and they won't be able

to keep from thinking of a thousand reasons why we didn't call.

We left them a map with the general area of Paul's cabin marked on it. Paul also marked the outpost, and the route we planned to take. It isn't completely accurate, but it'll give them a place to start, and a general search area. Please Lord, help them know how to find me!

Oh, how I hurt for them! I know how scared they'll be. I wish there were some other way for me to get home, and I wish I could be there by tomorrow morning.

I was so anxious I trembled inside. I told myself each day that I couldn't let it stop me from doing what I must do, just in case my rescue took a lot longer than I hoped it would. I knew that I must make some type of signal for when they came looking for us. It had to be built so that the boys would recognize it without question. They would know, without a doubt, that it was something I had done to mark our location. I also had to search for a place to make a bonfire. I knew the beach area close to the edge of the river would be the best spot, but I was afraid to build it there just in case those men came back. I knew in my heart that those men were gone, but I still couldn't let my guard down.

I knew that Bo would let me know if they were there and I knew that I would be able to defend myself and shoot them if I had to, but that area still made me nervous. So, I decided to build the bonfire by the boulders above the beach. This area was closer to the woods, closer to my cabin, and the woodpile could be mistaken for a pile of driftwood. "Please, God, help me to be patient," I prayed. "I feel as if I'm going to explode at any moment because I'm so anxious! I must not let myself get too nervous." I knew it could be weeks before the boys found me *if* they found me. I wouldn't allow myself to dwell on those thoughts, though, because they would keep me from doing all the things I needed to do to get prepared.

Chapter 42

Dear Diary

September 2
The main thing I have to do is to make sure I have plenty of wood cut and ready for winter. I've been cutting and stacking it all summer, but I still don't know if it'll be enough. When I first started cutting it, I had to measure each cut to make sure could it wasn't longer than eighteen inches because anything bigger won't fit in my camp stove. Now, I can just eyeball it and know that it'll fit. I also left some of the wood longer so I can use it in my outside fire pit when the weather permits. I've stacked the wood all along the outside walls and the inside walls of the cabin. Having the wood right up next to the walls has made my vole problem worse, but I'd rather have voles than to have to go away from the cabin for wood when the snow comes.

I've thought about trying to build a fireplace knowing that my little camp stove might not be enough to keep the cabin warm. I'd already gathered rocks and made a hearth on the back wall of the cabin. But I'm just not sure what to do the next. I knew I must cut out part of the wall and build a firebox inside and the rest outside of the cabin. I've thought about moving my camp stove out of the tent and into the cabin, but I really don't want to do that. I'm so tired! I don't know if I have the strength to do any more building, and I just don't really know what to do for the mortar or flue. I don't think the mud and moss will hold although the chinking seems to be holding. But, when I build a fire, would it just catch fire and burn? Whatever I decide, I can't do it now because it's started raining almost every day now and it actually has been for nearly two weeks. It's not very hard but it's continuous. So, for now, the fireplace will just be something I'll have to think about.

It's so hard to do any work outside. Not only is it raining, but it's turned much colder. I guess winter will be here sooner than I had thought. I don't want to think about spending the winter in Alaska! "Please, Lord! I want to be home when winter comes!"

I can't bear the thought of not being at home for Christmas. Just the thought of it makes me want to cry. The weather has me so depressed all I want to do is climb into the bed, pull the covers over my head, and stay there until someone comes to rescues me. But I know that I can't give into those thoughts. It'll do no good, and it'll only make me feel sorrier for myself than I already do.

Chapter 43

We heard wolves as we were headed back to the cabin after a day of working on my signals. They sounded far away, but Bo still threw up his head and answered their call before I could stop him. I grabbed him, put my hand around his nose, and scolded him. I told him that he couldn't do that anymore. What if they heard him, they might come here! We'd heard them before, but Bo had paid them no attention. They always sounded like they were very far away. This time though, they seemed much closer. "Oh, please, please, please don't let the wolves hear Bo! And please, please, please don't let them come this way!" I prayed. After hearing the wolves, and even though it was almost dark, I picked up my rifle, the water buckets, and anything else I had empty that would hold water, loaded it on the sled, and went to the spring. I filled everything with as much water as I could. I wanted to be prepared just in case. Our ordeal with the wolverine and the bear, had taught me to be more cautious. If wolves came to the cabin, we might have to stay inside until they left. It could be several days before we could get out and get more water, so I wasn't going to take any chances this time.

I let Bo go with me, but I had him on his leash. Poor Bo, he thought he had done something wrong. He just sat down, looked at me, and hung his head every time I stopped to listen. I kept looking around, with my binoculars hoping I would be able to see them before they saw us. Moving as quickly as possible, I filled the buckets and tins and hurried back to camp. I moved everything I thought I would need inside the cabin just to be on the safe side. It had gotten dark and we hadn't heard them again. I was very nervous and tense. I jumped at every little sound. I was so scared that I could barely sit still, even though Bo didn't seem to be bothered at all. He just lay there sleeping peacefully. Oh, how I wished I could feel that secure.

I had to finish building the signal fire, for my rescue, wolves or no wolves. I dragged some of the tops from the trees that I had cut down earlier to the area by the boulders where I had decided to build a fire. I'm glad that I chose this area because there was already a good size pile of driftwood and debris here. I could shove the tops under some of the pile and throw the rest on top. It should catch and burn very quick despite the almost constant rain. Even though I was afraid of the wolves I knew I had to do this.

The bonfire was finished. I cut some kindling and soaked it in bear grease so it would light and burn quickly. I kept it and some matches on my table where I could grab them and run as soon as I heard anything that sounded like a plane or a boat. It took me most of one day to finish all this, but it was ready. The next day I put my signal stones on the boulders at each end of the beach. Whichever way they came from I knew they'd have to see them. I had to make these signals as big and obvious as I could. I prayed if the boys saw them, they'd know that they were signs from me. I hoped they'd remember all our camping trips and the mapping skills Paul taught us. I hoped they would remember that my sign was three stones stacked one on top of the other.

One of the boulders wasn't so hard to climb, but the one at the far end of the beach was much taller and went way back into the woods. I'd never been to the other end of it even though Bo and I had tried to find it several times. It wasn't hard to get the signal stones in place on the smaller boulder, but the other one took a lot of work. First, I took a ladder and put it against the boulder. Then, I climbed up to an outcropping and pulled myself the rest of the way up. Because the stones were so heavy, I had to use a pair of Paul's pants like a sling. I put a stone on them, tied the legs around the stones, then tied a rope around the pants, and tied the other end around my waist. Then, when I reached the top, I pulled them up. I had to make three trips because the stones were too big to bring up more than one at a time. Thank God, I only used three stones in my sign. I don't know if I would have had the strength to make any more trips up and down pulling the rocks up. "Please, Lord, let the boys remember my sign!"

We heard the wolves again last night, and they sounded much closer. When they started howling, I grabbed Bo and put my hand around his muzzle and held his mouth shut so he couldn't answer them. I told him, "No! No! You can't answer them! They might find us! They're not other dogs! They're wolves! They're not our friends!"

It felt like they howled for hours! Poor Bo was so upset he was trembling and whining, and it was breaking my heart, but I wouldn't let him go. I kept talking to him, rubbing him, holding him, telling him that he must not respond to their call.

Finally, it was over! Bo just lay on the floor and wouldn't even look at me. He didn't understand that what I had done was for his own good. "Please, God," I prayed, "make them go another way! Haven't we had enough to deal with? The wolverine held us captive for days! That bear just about finished me! And, now wolves! Lord! Please! Let the boys come and find us before the wolves do! Please!"

I was so afraid, but I couldn't stay inside forever. Bo and I had to go to the lookout every day because I couldn't chance missing a rescue boat. I was afraid to take Bo with me, but I knew I couldn't leave him in the cabin. I thought I'd be able to kill a wolf with my pistol if I had to, but I'd also always have my rifle with me. I hoped I would be able to protect us if the wolves came while we were out of the cabin. "Dear Lord, I beg you. Please help us!"

From the lookout, I could see everything I'd done to get ready to be rescued. Now, as I stood and looked at my signals, I wondered how I managed to climb the boulders and pull the stones all the way up to the top. I looked over to the bonfire and thought about the best place to light it. I prayed that the boys would see all of them and know that they were signals from me. I prayed that I heard them coming and could get the fire lit before they'd passed on by. I prayed that they came soon! I was so ready to go home!

Dear Diary

September 5
This waiting is killing me! I feel as if I'm going to come apart at the seams! I'm so

anxious that I cry at every little thing! I know Bo thinks I'm crazy, and maybe I am, but I can't seem to stop crying!

Going to the lookout had become our most important daily outside activity. As I turned to leave the lookout, I picked up the water buckets that I had brought with me, went to the spring and filled them with water, and headed back to camp. As we got inside the cabin, I unleashed Bo, but he immediately wanted to go back outside. That's when I heard the wolves! They were back and much closer this time! I grabbed Bo! I sat on the floor holding his mouth clamped tightly shut and told him to be quiet. He just kept wiggling and turning his head this way and that. He was listening, wanting to respond but I wouldn't let him. Suddenly, he lunged and broke free running away from me! I jumped up and tried to get a hold of him again! I screamed at him, "No Bo! No!" But, before I could get my hands on him, he raised his head, and howled! As he was howling, I grabbed him and clamped his mouth shut, but it was too late! I sat holding Bo's muzzle for the longest time waiting for a response from the wolves, but none came. After that it was so very quiet! We just sat there trembling and listening. I finally let Bo go. He immediately ran to the door and looked back at me whining. I knew he wanted outside, but I refused to let him go. He sniffed all around the cabin, and then he just went back and lay by the door. I knew he was pouting, but he'd just have to pout, because there was no way under heaven that we would've left the cabin that night.

I got up, built a fire, and started supper. I knew the damage was done. Bo refused to eat anything, so after I finished my supper, I got both guns, cleaned and loaded them, and set all my bullets the out on the table. I loaded my pockets with them making sure to put rifle shells on the left and the bullets for the pistol on the right. I just hoped I remembered which pocket to use when I needed to reload. I had to be ready, and that was all I knew to do. I continued sitting at the table checking and rechecking making sure I didn't forget anything. As I sat and watched Bo sleep, my heart was breaking because I knew if the wolves came and they had a chance they would kill him and probably me too. As tears ran down my cheeks, I covered my mouth to silence the sobs at that thought. As I reached out to touch the rifle, I could see that my hand was shaking. I had been terrified of the bear, but I was more terrified of the wolves. They were so silent I knew I'd never know they were there until it was too late. And I knew there would be more than one of them because they traveled in packs. They were so much bigger than Bo, I knew he wouldn't stand a chance if they got to him. "Oh, Merciful God, please help me save Bo."

I tried to go to bed, but I couldn't stay there. I put a little more wood in the stove and built up the fire. I pulled the coffee pot that I had prepared for the next morning, over the fire and made coffee. I knew there would be little or no sleep for me that night. I knew the wolves were close by. I could feel them. I kept jumping up at any noise from outside. I would grab the gun and creep to the door, look out of the slot, and try to see what had made the noise. I just knew that any minute it would be the wolves. I half hoped it would be them. I knew I was going to have to try to kill them, and I was ready to kill them just to get it over with. The anticipation was so unbearable I was trembling inside.

Chapter 44

The next morning, we had just finished breakfast when I heard the plane. I jumped up, grabbed the leash, and put it on Bo. Then I grabbed my little bundle of kindling from the table, put it and the matches in my pocket, grabbed the rifle, buckled the pistol around my waist, and ran for the beach. When we reached the beach, I immediately tried to start the bonfire.

All at once the wolves were there! They were so large! The lead wolf was huge and black! He would make three of Bo! In my excitement and haste to light the fire, I had forgotten all about them! I yanked Bo back by his leash, and grabbed his collar trying to hold on to him and trying to aim my rifle at the same time. I couldn't get a shot from this position, so I let go of Bo's collar, and held him by the leash so I could straighten up. I put my legs on either side of Bo, squeezing tight, trying to keep him as close to me as possible! He was so angry! He kept lunging, jumping, growling and snarling viciously! All at once, he pulled out of his collar and lunged at the closest wolf!

My God! There were four of them, and they were all trying to get to him! All I could think of was I must help Bo. Screaming and hollering I raised the rifle! I started to shoot but was so afraid I would hit Bo that I couldn't bring myself to squeeze the trigger! Instead of aiming into the middle of the pack, I fired two or three shots into the air hoping the shots would scare them off! Bo and the lead wolf were fighting so viciously, they didn't even notice the shots!

I had to help Bo! So, I lifted the rifle, took careful aim, and shot one of the wolves killing it! Thank God my aim was true! The other two ran into the woods, but they were only gone for a minute or two before they returned! This time they circled in from behind me. Screaming in fear and anger, I quickly turned to face them! I knew I had to stand my ground! I took careful aim and shot another one killing it instantly! I promptly fired again and wounded the other one as it ran into the woods! At that moment, I heard the plane again! It seemed to be right behind me, and I heard voices calling, but I couldn't take my eyes off Bo and the wolf! It had Bo down by the throat, and I knew I had to do something! Running forward, I aimed at the wolf's head and shot, praying that I didn't hit Bo! As the wolf fell away from Bo, I ran to him and frantically looked around to make sure the wounded wolf hadn't come back!

I dropped down beside him, and as I looked at his ripped and torn body, I knew he was dead! There was blood everywhere I touched! I picked him up, cuddled him in my arms, lay my head on his, and cried like I had done so many times these last few months. I told him how sorry I was, that it was my fault, how sorry I was that I couldn't save him, and how brave he was. I could hear the voices calling me, but I couldn't lift my head.

Chapter 45

All at once, Todd and Joey were there kneeling beside us and hugging us, but at that moment, nothing mattered except Bo! Oh, my poor little Bo! You were so brave and fearless! *Dear God, how could you allow this to happen?* I screamed in my head. *Bo was my dearest, bravest, most fearless companion! Why didn't you allow me to save him! Why, Lord, why!*

The boys kept apologizing, saying how sorry they were that they hadn't gotten there sooner to help me save him. We sat huddled together crying and talking over each other until the pilot, who Joey introduced as Andy, quietly asked if there was anything he could do to help. I just shook my head, as I took off my coat and began wrapping Bo in it. Todd offered to take him, but I wouldn't let him. I told them to follow me and to keep an eye out for the wolf I had wounded. Joey picked up my rifle, and Todd took the pistol, and then we started down the trail. When we reached the cabin, I lay Bo gently on the bed. It was all I could do not to collapse beside him. My strength was completely gone, and I felt as if my legs wouldn't hold me up another minute, so I knelt beside the bed and gently rubbed Bo's head as I started sobbing uncontrollably. I couldn't catch my breath. After a few minutes, both boys asked at once, "Mom, where's Dad?"

I turned from the bed and looked at them with tears streaming down my face. I had rehearsed this moment many, many times over the summer, but now that the time had come, I couldn't seem to find the right words to tell the boys what had happened. I took a moment while getting up from beside the bed to try to find the best way to tell them. I slowly made my way to the table and sat down. With a sob in my voice, I reached out and took their hands, and slowly told them that Paul was dead. I told them what had happened and even though I had tried with everything I had, there was nothing I could do to save him. Todd just stood staring at me while Joey dropped to the floor covered his face and began crying. He repeated over and over, "No, no, no, not Dad." I hope and pray that I never again have to tell anyone that their father is dead! Finally, Todd dropped down beside me and hugged me. Through his tears, he said, "Oh, Mom, I'm so sorry you had to be here alone when that happened." Then they both started asking questions. "When did Dad die? How were you able to bury him by yourself? How did you survive all alone out here?" When they had run out of questions, I told them that I would explain everything and take them to his grave.

As we were talking, Andy, the pilot, came and joined us by the table. He said, "I tried everything I could to revive Bo, but nothing worked, He's gone. I'm sorry, but there was nothing else I could do." With the boys beside me, we went back to the bed. As I sank to the floor, the boys knelt beside me. Through tears, I kept saying, "Oh my brave little Bo, I'm so sorry. This is all my fault. If I hadn't insisted we bring you with us you would still be alive. They wrapped their arms around me and kept assuring me that Bo had done what he was supposed to do. We stayed by the bed for a long time, but eventually I knew that we were only putting off the inevitable. We had to bury Bo, and it would never get any easier, so I gathered him up, wrapped him in his blanket, and I led them to Paul's grave. We buried Bo next to Paul.

Chapter 46

As we were gathered by the graves, Andy said he would stay and help the boys work on the boat motor, but he couldn't stay more than a day because he had other flights he must make. I just stood there looking at the boys with tears running down my face, then with a tremble in my voice, I blurted out, "I can't go with you! I can't leave Paul and Bo here! I can't bring myself to go without them!" With shocked looks on their faces, both said at once, "Are you crazy Mom? You must come with us! There's no way we're going to leave you here! Dad would tell you you should go home! Dad would never let you stay in this place all alone! You have to come with us! We need you, Mom! You can't stay here!"

As I listened to the boys, I could hear Paul saying, "Now, Julie, you know you have to go home. Your job here is done. The boys and Amy need you. You are my brave Julie girl, and you can handle this. Now be strong and do what needs to be done."

As I stood there looking down at the graves, I knew I would always feel guilty. I knew if I had made different choices both Paul and Bo might still be alive. I knew when I left Alaska a part of me would always be here. It was buried in the graves of my two best friends, my husband Paul, the love of my life, and my brave and loyal companion Bo.

Chapter 47

With the help of Andy, the boys fixed the boat motor. After that was done, we started packing. Andy asked if he could skin the wolves for the hides. I told him that would be fine with me, and I asked if he would also like to have the wolverine and bear hides. He said he'd be glad to have them. That he could get a good amount of money for them both, especially the bear. "Where did you get them?" He asked. When I told him that I had killed them both, he and the boys just stopped and stared at me with a look of amazement on their faces, and their mouths hanging open.

After they were able to speak, they all started asking questions at once. So, I told them about killing the wolverine. I told them how he had been such an irritating little pest. How he had driven Bo crazy, and how I had sprained my ankle falling off the ladder. Then I told them how the bear had terrorized us for days before I had killed it. When I told them all the other things I had done, like cleaning the bear, smoking the meat, and making soap and candles from the fat, they just couldn't believe it. The boys just kept saying, "How did you do it, Mom?" They just kept saying over and over they wished they had been here to help me and how proud they were of me. I told them about having a good laugh when I pictured Joey's face while I was elbow deep in bear guts. I laughed again while I was telling them about it, and before I knew it, we were all doubled over laughing at the thought.

After we had had a good laugh, I told them I wouldn't have been able to do any of it if it hadn't been for Bo. That I would surely have gone crazy had I been by myself. That I thought I did what I did as much for Bo as I did for myself. Talking about Bo made us tear up all over again. I still couldn't believe he was really gone. After a few minutes, we finally managed to gather ourselves together and get back to packing up everything. We talked as we packed, and by the time we were finished for the day, I realized I had only told them a small amount of everything that had happened over the last few months.

While we were eating supper, Andy asked, "Mrs. Stone, why is your tent inside the cabin?"

"Because I built the cabin around the tent," I said with a laugh.

"What do you mean you build it?" Todd asked. "Isn't this Dad's cabin?"

"No, we never made it to that cabin," I answered.

Todd said, "Mom, you really built this? You're not kidding?"

I chuckled and said, "No, I'm not kidding, Todd, I built it. I knew I would need more than a tent because I was afraid that the tent wouldn't give us enough protection. I had first decided to just build walls around the tent, but after seeing the moose and the bear on the trail, and then the wolverine that kept trying to get in, I decided to put the roof on. I also decided that the roof was necessary because even though I was praying that you would come and rescue me before winter, I couldn't take the chance of not having something sturdier than the tent in the snow. So, I did what I had to do. You know me. When I set my mind to something, nothing will stop me. Although at times I thought the cabin would beat me."

The next morning, Andy said he was sorry, but he really had to leave. I asked him if he was flying back to the outpost. When he said yes, I told him about those two awful men that I had overheard. I told him that they had followed us with the intention of robbing us, sinking the boat, and leaving us stranded. When the boys heard this, they were horrified that I had had to go through such a terribly scary situation. Joey put his arms around me and hugged me while Todd got so mad it was all I could do to calm him down. He wanted to get his hands on them right then and there. Andy assured me that he would notify the authorities. He said that there had been quite a few unsolved robberies on the river over the last several years, and now that the authorities would have a description of the men, maybe they would be captured. He said that if they were still around, he would absolutely have them arrested. He also said that he hoped he found them first. He would make them sorry they ever even thought about harming such a fine family.

As he was preparing to leave, I hugged him and thanked him for everything he had done for us. I told him he would always have a special place in my heart and that we would never forget him. I made him promise to visit us if he was ever in the Seattle area. We sent him off with a good supply of bear jerky, smoked meat, lye soap, and the skins.

Chapter 48

We stayed several more days at the cabin after Andy left. He had offered to take us back with him, but we had decided that we would stay and pack everything up. The boat had to be returned to the outpost, and we needed time to say our goodbyes to Paul and Bo. We told him that we would find him if he were at the outpost when we arrived, and we'd hire him to fly us back to Anchorage.

The day after Andy left, the boys said they wanted to make sure the graves were more secure. They went to the boulders and found large stones to add to the ones I had put on Paul's grave. They cried again when they saw that I had placed his sign on the grave, and they made sure to replace it after they had added the larger stones. They covered Bo's grave just as well as they had Paul's and added my sign on his, stacking three stones one on top of the other. The boys said they would have never found us if they hadn't seen my signal on the large boulder. Joey said, "When we first saw it, Todd looked at me and said, 'Joey, did you see that? That had to be Mom and Dad!' We were so excited we almost made Andy lose control of the plane. We made Andy turn around and go back just so we could be sure we had really seen it. As we were headed back, we saw you, Bo, and the wolves! It was all Andy could do to keep us from jumping out of the plane! He was landing as fast as he could, but we couldn't wait. We jumped out before the plane ever even touched down. It's a wonder we didn't tear up Andy's plane, or break a leg or an arm. Oh, Mom! I wish we could have found you even just an hour earlier." He said, "Maybe we could have saved Bo if we'd been here just a little sooner."

I hugged both boys. "You can't dwell on that," I said. "Those wolves had been waiting on us to leave the cabin for days. That fight was going to happen at some point whether you were here or not. And I shudder to think what would have happened if you boys had gotten on the beach before us. The wolves might have attacked you. There were just too many of them. I know in my heart that Bo was doing exactly what he was supposed to do by protecting me. He was such a brave and faithful companion. I'll never forget everything he did to make this entire ordeal bearable."

We decided to only take my clothing and other necessary items back with us. We'd take enough food for a few days, and the small tent, but I told the boys that I wanted to leave everything else here. The boys said they wanted to take most of their dad's tools and guns back with them, and I told them they should take anything they wanted. I broke into tears again as I packed up Bo's collar and leash, and when I had to go through what was left of Paul's clothes.

We made sure all the food was packed in watertight tins. We stacked all the wood I'd cut inside the cabin so it would stay dry, and we even left the tent and camp stove in place. I wanted to make sure that if anybody else got stranded here, they'd have shelter and enough food for a week or two at least. I left a letter explaining what had happened. I also asked that they leave the cabin ready for the next person when they moved on.

Before we left, I wanted to show the boys all the places I'd discovered. As we got ready to go, I gave Todd Paul's rifle, Joey took mine, and I strapped on the pistol. I told them I never left the cabin without having at least one gun with me.

I took them to the spot where I'd cut the wood for the cabin. I pointed out the boulder that the bear had been sitting on. We all laughed at the image of me dragging Bo and running for dear life back to the cabin. Todd said, "The bear was probably thinking what in the world was that?"

Joey put his arm around my shoulder, and with tears in his voice, he said, "Oh, Mom."

We went to the spring, the berry patch, and the inlet. The boys laughed so hard, they just about fell over, when I told them about the moose eating my clothes. I took them to my lookout spot where I would stand and watch for those horrible men. I decided not to take them to my pretty little, glen. Even though I never visited it again, it was a special place that I couldn't share with anyone else. It helped me to show them all the places that had become mine. I realized that even though this had been a horrible ordeal, there were places there that would always bring sweet memories to mind when I thought about them.

Chapter 49

Dear Diary

September 10
Even though I prayed every day to be
rescued from this place, I never thought it
would be this hard for me to leave. It's
almost impossible for me to believe that I
had buried Paul and Bo in this place, and
now I have to leave them here! The boys
promised me that we would come back
next spring to take them home to be
properly buried, but that isn't helping me
any at this moment. I feel like my heart is
being ripped out of my chest! How can I
leave them here? "Oh Lord, I know that I
must leave, but I don't know how. Please
help me! Please give me the strength to do
this!"

As I stepped over into the boat, I could
almost hear Paul saying. "That's my Julie Girl."
So, with gritted teeth, I took my seat and said,
"Boys let's go home."

It only took us two days and a night to get
back to the outpost, and we found Andy waiting
for us there. After a short visit with the outpost

owner, I filled out a report explaining everything that had happened and where the cabin was. The next morning Andy flew us back to Anchorage. We picked up the car and spent one night in Anchorage before we left for home. Taking turns driving, we drove straight through stopping only when necessary. It only took half the time to get home.

Chapter 50

I should be overjoyed to be home.

Chapter 51

Amy was waiting for us at the house, and the moment she saw Todd, she threw herself at him. As he picked her up, she squealed, "We're going to have a baby!"

Todd just stopped in mid-spin, and looked at her, and asked, "What did you say?" Then, hugging her tightly, he began to laugh. He was jumping around, crying, and shouting like he did when he got his first bicycle. When they settled down, Amy apologized, saying she had planned to tell him over a romantic dinner for just the two of them but, when she saw him, she just couldn't wait.

I was so happy for them. Paul and I had always hoped to have grandchildren. It broke my heart to know that he would never get the opportunity to hold our first grandbaby or any grandbabies that we might be blessed with in the future. My tears of joy were mixed with just as many tears of pain and sorrow. Oh, how I wished Paul could be here for this. *Oh Lord,* I thought silently, h*ow am I supposed to handle all this? Please give me strength. I can't think about Paul right now. This is Todd and Amy's time, and I won't let his death spoil their excitement.*

I turned and looked up at the house. Slowly I climbed up the steps to the porch while the boys, with Amy's help, began to unload the car. They took all the camping gear we'd kept to the garage and stored it away. I just stood there looking at the door unable to turn the knob. Finally, with a shake of my head, I willed myself to reach forward and open the door.

It was all I could do to walk into the house that had been my home for years. As I entered the living room, I just stood and stared. It was like I'd never seen it before. I felt as if I didn't belong. Then all the anguish and grief returned. With tears running down my face, I grabbed up a vase and threw it with all my strength against the wall! As it shattered into pieces, I shouted, "Damn you, Paul! Damn you! Why didn't you tell me you were sick! You had to know that you might die! You had nitroglycerin for God's sake! They only give you that if it's the last thing they can do! Paul, why in God's name, didn't you trust me! I could've helped you!" While I shouted, I stomped around the room picking up things and throwing them as hard as I could. As I got to the bookcase, I froze. There I stood face to face with Paul's smiling face. With more rage than I ever knew I could have, I snatched up Paul's picture, and threw it with all my might to the floor! I began furiously stomping it! "What about me, Paul!" I cried, with venom in my voice. "How am I supposed to survive here without you! I hate you, Paul Stone! I hate you for what you did to us! I hate you! You knew you had no business taking a trip like that! You knew you could die, but no, we had to go to Alaska! You wanted to rebuild that damn cabin!

What happened, next Paul? What? You died! You left Bo and me there to survive the best way we could! Well, I did survive, Paul! But Bo didn't! I did everything I could, but I couldn't save him from the wolves! And it's your fault! It's entirely all your fault!" I sobbed as I collapsed into a chair and covered my face with my hands.

As I heard the kids come into the kitchen, I jumped up and told myself to stop crying. "Tears won't change what happened, and you've cried enough. It'll do no good. It never has." I quickly dried my face and hurried into the kitchen not wanting them to see the mess I'd made of the room.

As I entered the kitchen, Joey got a glimpse of the living room. He just stared and said, "Mom?" with a questioning look on his face. I just looked up at him, put my hand on his chest, and pushed him back into the kitchen. With a smile, I said, "Don't worry, I'll clean it up."

The boys and Amy settled around the kitchen table as I started a pot of coffee. The boys were telling Amy about the bear, and Amy kept exclaiming that they had to be lying. Joey said, "You tell her, Mom. Tell her it really did happen. You really did kill a bear!"

"I did," I said, as I came to join them at the table. "I was terrified, but I knew it was him or me, so I did what I had to do."

Amy just stared at me. "Really?" she asked.

"Yes really." I answered. "But I can't talk about all that right now. I'm much too tired to think about it. I'd much rather hear about you and my new grandbaby. How far along are you? Have you thought about names yet?"

Amy and Todd looked at each other and grinned. "We were going to ask you about that," Amy said. "Todd and I talked while we were unpacking the car, and we decided that if it's a boy, we'd really like to name him Paul. Is that ok with you?"

With tears in my eyes, I said, "That'll be wonderful, and Paul would be thrilled."

Chapter 52

I've been home for a week, and it still seems utterly unreal. I haven't been able to stay in our house for long periods of time. I can still feel Paul in everything, and I find myself constantly looking around for Bo. It seems that all I do when I'm here is walk from room to room touching things and crying. I think sometimes I'm going to lose my mind. All the memories and all the guilt I feel are almost unbearable because I know their deaths were partly my fault. I feel as if I'm in limbo. I'm stuck somewhere between here and my cabin in Alaska. I can still see the graves hidden in the woods above the beach. Each time I step into this house, I feel like they've died all over again.

We held a Memorial Service for Paul the Sunday after we came home. We'd planned for it to be a small service, but I think everyone in town came to pay their respects. It reminded me how much Paul was loved and respected. It was very touching, and I truly appreciated the outpouring of love and support, but I felt utterly empty. I thought I would go crazy with all the questions and sympathy from friends and advice on how to cope with my loss. I wanted to stand up and tell everyone how selfish he really was.

How he'd brought this on himself. But I wouldn't. It would only hurt the boys and wouldn't change a thing.

I've been staying at the farm with Mom and Dad since I returned. I know that they're worried about me, but for now, I can't stay in my own home. I think that I may sell the house. I know the boys won't be happy, but I hope they'll understand. Maybe, if I start all over, I can get over these feelings of guilt and loss. I haven't talked to them about it yet. Maybe I'm a coward, but I just can't do it yet.

Mom assured me that Paul's and Bo's deaths were not my fault, that we all have our time to die, and that it's on God's time. If it weren't God's will, they wouldn't have died when they did. I know in my head that she is right, but I just can't let go of the guilt not only for Paul but also for Bo.

Chapter 53

A few days after I'd gotten home, I made an appointment to see Paul's physician. I had to know just how long Paul had had a bad heart and why he hadn't told me. The doctor told me that Paul had had a heart problem for years but had refused to take any medication for it. This year, when the doctor had seen Paul, he told him that his heart was a lot worse, and if he should have a heart attack, it would probably be fatal. That's when he agreed to get the nitroglycerin prescription filled. When I asked the doctor why on earth he hadn't told me, he simply said, "Paul, didn't want you to know. And because he was my patient, I wasn't allowed to tell you."

I didn't think I could get so furious with Paul again! I felt so betrayed! How could he keep this from me for all these years? Why had I not realized that he had a heart problem? How had he kept it from me? What did he think I would do? All the questions came rushing in as I stalked from the doctor's office to the hardware store getting madder with every step I took. I had to know if Todd knew, or if Paul had kept it from him, too.

Chapter 54

As I stormed into the hardware store, there stood Todd talking to old man Peters, the biggest old gossip in town. Todd was just smiling and nodding his head out of politeness. I'm sure he wasn't really listening to anything old man Peters was saying. As I stormed by them, I said, "Todd, I need to talk with you." I hurried into the office without so much as good morning to Mr. Peters. They both stood and stared after me, and Todd politely said, "Excuse me, Mr. Peters," as he turned and asked, "Mom, what's wrong?" while following me into the office closing the door behind him.

He could see I was mad to the boiling point. I stood there for just a moment catching my breath, and then I slowly turned to ask him, "Todd, did you know your father had a bad heart?" As I stood there waiting for an answer, I knew he'd known. He looked like a little boy with his hand caught in the cookie jar.

He said, "I caught Dad taking the nitroglycerin one time, just before the wedding and asked him why he was taking it. He just laughed it off telling me not to worry about it. He said everything was fine, and I was sure you knew about it, so I didn't even think to mention it to you." As I stood there looking at Todd, I wished he were a little boy again so I could give him a good whipping, but looking at his face, I knew he had whipped himself enough. As the anger left me, I put my arms around Todd's waist and told him I understood, but what I didn't understand was why his dad felt like he couldn't trust any of us. Todd and I stood hugging each other for a long time. As my anger died away, I felt a little of the guilt go with it. Maybe my mom was right, we only die when God is ready for us, and nothing I could have done would have changed that.

Epilogue

Today's Saturday. I've been home for several weeks now, and I've finally come to terms with Paul's death. I know in my heart that he would've never intentionally put us in any danger. These weeks have been really hard, but after much soul searching and prayer, I've decided to try to stay in our house. There are more good memories here than bad, and even though I still have days when I have to get away, it's getting easier. I've been filling my time working with the poor bag ladies just like I promised Paul and God I would.

Late that Saturday evening, the boys, Amy, and I were sitting on the porch. We sat in companionable silence just as Paul and I had done so many times over the years. As I glanced up, I saw our neighbor, Carol, who lives a couple of doors down, headed our way. She was carrying a large box, and I quietly asked Joey to go put the coffee on.

"Carol's bringing in another cake," Todd whispered. "I hope this one's chocolate." Amy playfully hit his arm and told him to hush.

As Carol came up on the porch, she walked over to me and set the box down at my feet. With a smile, she said, "I think this belongs to you."

Giving Carol a puzzled look, I lifted the top off the box and looked inside. There, looking up at me was a little, gray, fuzzy face with a tiny, black, straggly beard and big, brown eyes. His expression seemed to say, *where have you been? I've been waiting for you!* With tears in my eyes, I smiled and gently picked him up. I buried my face in his soft, furry, little neck just like I had done so many times with his dad, Bo.

THE END

About the Author

Jeanette Basson is 75 years old, and a new author. She's finally taken the time for herself to finish at least one of the many writing projects she's started over the years. She lives in Columbus, Mississippi with her Husband James. They've been married for 56 years. She has three grown children, a lovely Daughter-In- Law, and one Granddaughter. She loves art. Writing and painting called her name first and she practiced that for many years. She's tried her hand at many other forms of art, but she always came back to writing and painting. Her family and church have always been her first love, and they always will be.

She wants to make sure that everyone knows that there is no excuse for not following whatever dream you may have. You're never too old, too slow, too, busy, too uneducated, or too whatever. Those are all just lies that we tell ourselves to keep us from using whatever talent The Lord has given us.

She gives all the glory to God for the many gifts He has given her.